ERICA SPINDLER
Baby Mine

Silhouette Special Edition

Published by Silhouette Books New York

America's Publisher of Contemporary Romance

For the brave and loving woman
who gave me my heart's treasure.

To the gang at Plantation Coffeehouse:
Thanks for the information, the occasional I.O.U., and
most importantly, for the great cappuccinos and the quiet
place to put it all in order.

SILHOUETTE BOOKS
300 East 42nd St., New York, N.Y. 10017

BABY MINE

Copyright © 1992 by Erica Spindler

ISBN: 0-373-09728-X

First Silhouette Books printing March 1992

Printed in the U.S.A.

"Congratulations, Mrs. Adler— it's a girl!"

the woman from the adoption agency exclaimed through the telephone receiver. "You have a baby daughter. Big blue eyes, a cap full of dark curls, ten fingers and ten toes. I'll bring her to your home the day after tomorrow."

A baby daughter! Maggie was a mother! She had a daughter. A baby. Joy bloomed inside her. She smiled, then laughed and hugged herself.

The woman, obviously used to shocked silences, rambled on. "I know you have a lot of preparations to make between now and then, so I won't keep you. But I do look forward to meeting you and your husband the day after tomorrow. We'll be there at ten o'clock. Goodbye for now."

Maggie's smile suddenly faded. Her stomach crashed to her toes, her joy with it. Royce. Her *husband*. The husband from whom she was separated....

Dear Reader,

Welcome to Silhouette **Special Edition**... welcome to romance. Each month, Silhouette **Special Edition** publishes six novels with you in mind—stories of love and life, tales that you can identify with—romance with that little "something special" added in.

And this month has some wonderful stories in store for you. Lindsay McKenna's *One Man's War* continues her saga that is set in Vietnam during the sixties— MOMENTS OF GLORY. These powerful tales will capture you from the first page until the last! And we have an exciting debut this month—Debbie Macomber begins her new series, THOSE MANNING MEN. Don't miss the first book—*Marriage of Inconvenience*— Rich and Jamie's story.

Rounding out March are more stories by some of your favorite authors: Mary Curtis, Erica Spindler, Pamela Toth and Pat Warren. It's a wonderful month for love!

In each Silhouette **Special Edition** novel, we're dedicated to bringing you the romances that you dream about—stories that will delight as well as bring a tear to the eye. And that's what Silhouette **Special Edition** is all about—special books by special authors for special readers!

I hope you enjoy this book and all of the stories to come!

Sincerely,

Tara Gavin
Senior Editor
Silhouette Books

ERICA SPINDLER

came to writing from the visual arts and has numerous one-person, invitational and group exhibitions to her credit. She still teaches art classes in addition to her writing. "It seems only natural to me that I should be writing romance," says Erica. "My paintings had the same spirit of optimism and romanticism that my stories do."

A descendant of Marie Duplessis, who was the most famous courtesan of her day and the inspiration for Dumas's work *Camille,* Erica lives with her husband in New Orleans, where she does most of her writing in a penthouse that affords a panoramic view of that intriguing, history-rich city.

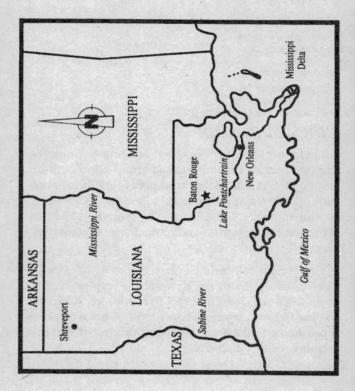

Chapter One

Sometime during the night, the rain had ended. The front had moved through, bringing cooler, dryer air that little resembled the soupy stuff southern Louisiana had been plagued with for most of the fall.

Even so, a thick fog hung over Lake Pontchartrain, and Maggie Ryan Adler stood on her veranda, staring out at the fog and at the light that glimmered on the horizon.

Would today be the day she took the first step toward the end?

Turning away from the lake and her thoughts, Maggie hugged her cardigan tighter around herself and started across the lawn toward what had once been the main residence's guest cottage and now housed A

Coffee and Pastry Place, the coffeehouse she owned with her oldest sister, Louise.

Maggie picked her way along the path between the buildings. Leaves from the moss-draped oaks littered the walkway, as did pine straw and petals from the last of the summer annuals. The storm had been a doozy. Rain had slashed against her roof and windows; the wind had bent the branches of the ancient oaks outside her bedroom. Normally she loved the sounds of a storm, enjoyed the flash of lightning and the rumble of thunder. Normally she would have slept like a baby and awakened refreshed and eager for the new day.

But nothing had been normal for a long time now, and instead of sleeping she had walked the floors until the wee hours—thinking of Royce, wishing and regretting.

With a small shake of her head, Maggie climbed the stairs of the raised cottage she and Louise had chosen to paint the softest of pinks. Looking back, she knew, was for fools, as was wasting life on regrets. She had to accept that there were things she would never have.

With an all-too-familiar ache in her chest, Maggie took one last look at the lake and the shimmer of sun on the horizon. She wasn't ready to let go, though. Not of her dreams, not of Royce.

Swallowing against the emotion that clogged her throat, she crossed the coffeehouse's wide front porch and unlocked the door. After disengaging the alarm and switching on the lights, she started brewing coffee.

The morning would be busier than usual. Until the fog began to burn off, the state police would convoy the cars across the causeway that connected the bedroom community of Mandeville to New Orleans. Some commuters would attempt to wait out the fog; others, knowing they had an excuse to be late for work, would linger over another cup of coffee or second pastry.

With that in mind, Maggie began to gather together the items she would need to restock the buffet.

"You should keep the doors locked until you're ready to open. Anyone could walk in."

Maggie whirled around, a hand to her throat. "Royce," she murmured, struggling to keep a tremor out of that one word.

"Maggie," he repeated evenly and without any evidence of the turmoil she felt. "You look surprised to see me."

She inched her chin up a notch, even though she knew the defensive gesture would be perceived as a sign of weakness. "Shouldn't I be?"

He didn't answer, but instead lifted his eyebrows in the way he always had when they'd argued—coolly and almost imperceptibly. It made her as crazy now as it had during the five years they'd lived together as husband and wife.

Moving from the doorway, he shrugged out of his trench coat and crossed toward her. His pearl gray suit was Italian, as no doubt were his tie, shirt and shoes. But he wore them comfortably and without artifice, as if he'd been born wearing Giorgio Armani originals.

In a way he had. As far as New Orleans's first families went, the Adlers were as well-placed as they came. His mother was a descendent of the famed *"filles à la cassette,"* his father a prominent politician. Between the two branches of the family, they owned three of the city's top ten restaurants, no small feat in a town known for the excellence of its dining establishments. And one celebrated by a star status within the society circle.

But family name and expensive clothing didn't make the man, and in Royce's case, they didn't have to. His looks were clean-cut but endlessly complicated, heart-stoppingly handsome without being anything but totally masculine. He exuded confidence, intelligence and the kind of sexuality that had emptied her head of everything she'd learned about relationships and about the dos and don'ts between the haves and have-nots.

Dammit, even now her knees were turning to putty, her heart to a drum. Hadn't she learned anything? Furious with herself, she folded her arms across her chest and scowled at him. "What do you want, Royce?"

He laughed softly and leaned against the counter. "You never used to be so direct."

"And you used to be quite direct."

"Touché." He lowered his head for a moment and his wheat-colored hair tumbled across his forehead. She caught herself a moment before she reached up to smooth it back.

Maggie slipped her hands into her pockets. "So, what *are* you doing here, Royce? Checking on your investment?"

He met her eyes, the expression in his inscrutable. "Maybe I wanted to say good morning to my wife."

She sucked in a sharp breath. "We ceased being husband and wife a long time ago."

"Did we?"

"You walked out!"

"You left me no other choice."

Angry words jumped to her tongue and she swallowed them. When they'd lived together he'd won every battle, every round—because he battled with reason, she with emotion.

That hadn't changed. But she had. She tipped her chin up. She would no longer give him the opportunity to win. "You don't have to worry about your money. Business is good."

"I never worried about...money."

For a moment Maggie thought she saw uncertainty, even vulnerability, in the fathomless blue of his eyes. And in that moment, her heart skipped a beat.

She called herself a fool. "Easy not to worry, isn't it? When you have so much."

"I'm sure," he said, straightening, "that business is fine. After all, you haven't asked for anything."

She curled her fingers into her palms. "And I won't. Not ever. I don't want your money, Royce. I never did."

"What did you want, Maggie?" he asked softly, meeting her gaze once more. "I don't think I know anymore."

Maggie stared at him, memories barreling over and into her. Memories of sleepy mornings wrapped together in the tangle of sheets, of long walks and shared secrets, of stolen kisses and whispered wishes.

Tears for those early days, for what they'd lost, burned the back of her eyes, and she glanced quickly away. "If you have to ask, I guess ... I don't know, either."

Royce muttered an oath. "This came to the restaurant."

Maggie looked at the envelope he held out. It was from one of the adoption agencies she'd listed them with. "You didn't open it?"

"Should I have?"

She made a sound of pain, dry and tight and hurting. She snatched the envelope from him, curling her fingers around the paper, crumpling it. "I guess not."

"You haven't told them about the change in our marital status?"

"No."

"Why not, Maggie?"

She couldn't meet his too-direct gaze, and she dropped her own to the envelope. What could she tell him? That to do so would be to admit to another what she couldn't even admit to herself? Or that she wasn't ready to let go and move on? He would never understand that. He had gone on without pause.

The truth of that hurt more than anything else.

"I haven't gotten around to it," she said finally, lamely.

"It's been almost nine months."

Nine months. It seemed like an eternity; it seemed like yesterday. She shook her head, fighting the tears. She wouldn't cry in front of him. Not now, not ever again.

"Maggie?"

She turned at the sound of Louise's voice. The other woman stood in the doorway, her carrot red hair curling wildly about her face, her fair skin reddened from the cool breeze.

"It was my morning to open up and yours to sleep in," Louise said, her concerned gaze moving from Maggie to Royce.

"I know," Maggie returned, her voice thick with tears. "I thought...because of the fog...you'd be late...." Her voice trailed off as her sister turned toward Royce and glared at him.

"Hello, Louise," he said easily, inclining his head. "How are you?"

"Fine."

"Joe and the kids?"

She crossed her arms over her chest. "Fine."

"Give them my regards." He slipped back into his coat and started for the door, stopping when he reached it. He looked back at Maggie and her heart constricted at the quiet determination, the finality, in his expression. "Goodbye, Mags."

For a full ten seconds both women stared at the empty doorway, then Maggie sagged against the counter, the tears she'd fought letting Royce see filling her eyes.

"You okay, sis?"

Maggie laughed, the sound shaky and anything but amused. "No. But I will be." Someday, she added silently. Shattered dreams took awhile to heal.

"I worry about you."

"You don't need to." Maggie smiled weakly. "I'm going to be all right. Really."

"I know, I know...." Louise slipped out of her coat and hung it on the coat tree just inside the door. "You're a survivor, you've told me before. But you're also my kid sister."

Maggie recognized Louise's tone too well. Annoyance warred with affection. "Don't start, Louise."

"I already have. Too many years ago to stop now." She caught Maggie's hand. "You're not sleeping well, are you?"

Maggie sighed. Louise—like the rest of the Ryan clan—simply did not understand the concept of minding one's own business. "No, but—"

"You need to have fun again," Louise said crisply. "You need to get out with people. Joe knows this great guy—he could fix you up."

Maggie groaned. "Absolutely not. A date is the last thing I want. Or need." She shook her head. "Thanks for thinking of me, sis, but no thanks."

Louise let out her breath in a frustrated huff. "You're an outgoing person, Maggie. You've always enjoyed being with people and... and it's not natural for you to spend so much time alone."

"I don't." Maggie began refilling the sugar baskets. "I have you, Alice and the rest of the family—which you have to admit is considerable. It's only my nights I spend alone, and there's no one else I want.... And that's the way I intend to keep it."

Louise frowned, obviously deciding to retreat for the time being. "Have the pastries arrived yet?"

Maggie set the baskets on the buffet, then collected the cocoa and cinnamon shakers to refill. "No. They're probably going to be late because of the weather. And there's not much on the day-old rack."

"So, what did he want?"

Maggie shot her an amused glance. "Was that your idea of stealth?"

Louise sniffed and filled the cream pitchers. "Not at all, I'm just—"

"Nosy."

"Concerned."

"He brought me this." Maggie handed her sister the crumpled envelope. "It came to Sassy's."

"It's from Associated Charities," Louise murmured, drawing her eyebrows together. "And you haven't opened it?"

"What's the point? Even if there were a baby available, they wouldn't give to me, not with me and Royce living apart."

"I'm sorry, Maggie." Louise crossed to where she stood and covered her hand with her own. "I know how badly you wanted a child."

Wanted? Maggie looked away, nonchalance, even forced, an impossibility. If only her need to be a mother *would* become a part of her past. If only it didn't hurt so damn bad every time she thought of a life without children.

"I've upset you."

Maggie looked back at Louise, blinking against the tears. She'd cried enough in the past eight and a half months to fill Lake Pontchartrain; the time had come to stop.

She drew in a deep breath. "It's not your fault, Louise. Yes, it hurts. But what am I supposed to do? I've got nine nieces and nephews and another one on the way. Should I move away? And even if I did, it hurts whenever I see children. What do I do about that? I can't stop living."

"No, but..." Louise paused a moment, then plowed on. "But you *can* do something about your marriage."

"Not now," Maggie said sharply, easing her hand from her sister's. "Our first customers are going to be strolling in any minute and we're not ready."

"They can wait." Louise caught her fingers again. "You were right. You can't stop living. But you have. It's been nearly nine months since you and Royce separated. Don't you think it's time to see a lawyer? Don't you think it's time to start on the next part of your life?"

The part without Royce.

Pain curled through her at the thought, and she met her sister's concerned gaze. "I can't, Louise. Not yet. Please try to understand, I just . . . can't."

"I hate to see you this way. I just wish—" Louise sucked in a sharp breath. "Royce Adler makes me so damn mad I could..." She shook her head. "He's such an iceberg!"

Maggie opened her mouth to deny her sister's words, then realizing what she was about to do, snapped it shut. Even after all this time, she wanted to defend him, to believe in him.

"It's more complicated than that," Maggie murmured after a moment. "You shouldn't blame Royce. This isn't his fault."

Louise tossed her head back. "It's not complicated, and I do blame him. He made you unhappy."

"We made each other unhappy," Maggie corrected softly, looking past her sister to the sun glittering on the horizon. "I wasn't the right woman for him."

Dammit. Royce scowled at the fog and at the line of cars in front of him. He flexed his fingers on the steering wheel, tamping back impatience and the urge to depress the accelerator and fly across the remaining miles of causeway.

And get as far away from Maggie as fast as possible.

As if mere miles could make him forget. Royce tightened his fingers on the steering wheel and inched his way across with the other cars. She wore the same fresh, fruity scent she always had; it tickled his senses still, conjuring memories best forgotten, memories of the dark and husky laughter, of the light and throaty cries.

And of the kind of warmth that had surrounded and filled him, the kind he'd never known before. Royce steeled himself against the ache, derided himself for his own imagination. But the ache, like a long, thin, cold blade, sliced through him anyway.

For a moment he'd had everything—he'd had the impossible, the fantasy.

Now all he had was . . . now.

Royce cursed under his breath. *Why had he gone to see her?* To deliver a piece of junk mail he could have forwarded or dropped in her box? He almost laughed out loud. That, even from a man whose actions of late represented a complete departure from good sense, was ludicrous.

So, why *had* he gone? It was over. It had been since the morning she'd delivered her ultimatum. Maybe before. What he'd thought they shared had been an illusion of his own making. For a short time he had convinced himself not only that love existed, but that it could be given freely and without strings.

He'd been a fool to believe such nonsense. Everything in life had conditions; there was always a catch. It had just taken him a lot longer to see Maggie's.

But he saw now, so why did he continue to be drawn back to her? Why did he feel sixteen years old, awkward and uncertain, when he looked at her? His ever-blunt sister, Honoria, had looked at him the other day and suggested he get a girlfriend.

He curled his fingers tighter around the wheel. Another woman was the last thing on his mind.

The high rises that flanked the lake at the end of the causeway loomed up before him, and Royce followed the line of cars off the bridge, then muttered several curt words as he saw he wouldn't be going any faster on the interstate than he had on the bridge.

He flipped on the radio. The traffic reporter made an obnoxious joke comparing motorists to flies stuck on glue paper; disgusted, Royce flipped it back off.

This kind of traffic had never bothered Maggie. Instead of becoming impatient or angry, she would have used the opportunity to admire the blue of the sky or the feel of the breeze. If they'd been together, she would have distracted him with an amusing story from her past or by engaging him in a discussion about something totally irrelevant to them or their lives.

Royce shook his head in an attempt to drive her from his thoughts. He concentrated on the restaurant, on the problems he and Honoria were having with their temperamental head chef, on the busy holiday season right around the corner, on anything but the woman who had, for a brief time, made him believe in . . . everything.

It didn't work. No matter how he tried, thoughts of Maggie shoved all others aside. Sighing, he gave in to the need and remembered the first time he saw her. She'd been wearing a bright white T-shirt and tight blue jeans. Her mane of wavy black hair had been pulled back with a loosely tied scarf, but long tendrils had escaped, making her look like a gypsy.

He shook his head, his lips lifting at the memory. She'd sneaked past the maître d', determined to see one of Sassy's owners about ordering her pastries for the restaurant. She'd been told nicely over the phone—three times—that Sassy's didn't use outside vendors for food products and that all their desserts were made in-house by their chef.

But Maggie was five feet two inches of pure determination. So she'd sneaked in with a piece of her best chocolate cake tucked inside her huge handbag.

The cake had been moist and sinfully rich. She'd named it, appropriately, Chocolate Ecstasy. He ordered a dozen—then he asked her out.

She'd been as surprised as he. By the invitation and her own acceptance of it.

Royce shook his head, staring blindly at the traffic light, seeing instead Maggie as she'd been that first day—flushed and amused and . . . vibrant. There had been something about her—hell, there still was. It was as if warmth radiated from her, from her smile and her eyes. The people of his acquaintance were never so open, never so enthusiastic.

And they never, ever wore their hearts on their sleeves.

Royce started as a horn blared behind him. The light had changed; the traffic in front of him had eased. He depressed the accelerator and raced away from his memories.

It was after noon when their last customer waved goodbye and stepped outside. Maggie rolled her shoulders and groaned, feeling every minute of the sleepless night before.

"We sold enough cappuccino and espresso to keep all of Mandeville awake." Louise hoisted a tray of dirty dishes and carried them to the dishwasher. "The Big Guy's dispenser even needs to be refilled," she added, referring to their huge copper-and-brass cappuccino maker.

"I'll take care of it." Maggie crossed to the bins containing the coffee beans they also sold by the pound. She began measuring out the appropriate amount of espresso beans needed to refill the dispenser.

"Is Alice relieving you?" Louise asked, referring to the teenager Maggie had taken in right after Royce had left.

"Mmm, at one o'clock. After she gets out of class." Maggie looked up from the beans. "She's doing well, don't you think?"

"Seems to be."

Maggie heard the doubt in her sister's voice but ignored it. Taking Alice in had been totally her decision—everyone, including Royce, had advised her against it. In fact, Alice had been the subject of her and Royce's last terrible fight.

Frowning, Maggie pushed that memory resolutely away and instead thought of the progress the girl had made in these past months. She was off the streets and back in school. At first only because of Maggie's insistence. Now Alice went willingly, some days it seemed even enthusiastically. And the girl had begun opening up, the destructive chip on her shoulder seeming to shrink a bit.

Maggie smiled and dropped the oversized scoop back into the bin. At least she'd made the right decision in one area of her life.

"Why don't you go ahead and go. I can handle it."

Maggie looked at her sister, lifting her eyebrows in question. "Where did that come from?"

"You just yawned."

"I did?"

"Mmm. You've been doing it all morning." Louise gestured toward the door. "Go ahead. Alice will be here any minute and we're not busy."

Maggie looked longingly at the clock, then back at her sister. "I'll wait. Like you said, it'll only be a few more minutes."

One became two, and still no Alice. Maggie stood in a patch of sunlight that tumbled through the large French-style windows and dappled the pine flooring with sunshine. She shoved her hands into the wide front pocket of her white apron and peered out at the street.

Where was she? Maggie nervously checked her watch. The teenager had come far in the past months, but she was still susceptible to influences that could drag her into trouble. Big trouble. Her new boyfriend was one of those influences. If only Alice could see him for what he was. If only—

"What that girl needs is a spanking."

Maggie whirled around. "Louise!"

"She knows she's scheduled for one o'clock, she knows you're expecting her." Her sister shook her head. "She's no doubt off gallivanting with her friends, no thought for how tired—or worried—you might be.''

Maggie shook her head at her sister's words. She couldn't help thinking that if the fates had taken a different turn, if there had been no Eileen and Billy Ryan, she herself could have been Alice. "Give her some time, Louise. She hasn't had anyone who cared enough to teach her about responsibility and obligations. It's going to take a while.''

Even as she finished uttering the words, tires squealed in the parking lot, followed by footsteps racing up the stairs and across the porch. Alice and...the boyfriend, Maggie thought, swallowing her disappointment. She turned slowly to face her ward, her admonishments dying on her tongue as she did. "Alice?'' she murmured, shocked.

"Sorry I'm late." Although the teenager inched her chin up defiantly, her eyes didn't quite meet Maggie's.

Maggie cleared her throat. Alice's hair, this morning an attractive, shoulder-length brown bob, was now as short as a boy's and cut in uneven spikes. Its color Maggie could only liken to cheap red wine. At a total loss, she cleared her throat again.

"You have something to say?'' Alice asked, tipping up her chin a bit more.

Maggie saw beyond the girl's cocky "so what" tone of voice, and her heart wrenched. Alice had such deep vulnerabilities, such a need for approval. It was there in the brightness of her eyes, the line of her jaw, and the way she folded her arms protectively over her chest.

Maggie swallowed her lecture. She untied her apron and slipped out of it, saying with what she hoped was nonchalance, "I tried to dye my hair red once. It turned green."

Louise laughed and the line of Alice's jaw softened. In Alice's eyes, Maggie read the thanks the girl hadn't come far enough to verbalize.

"She cried for a week," Louise said dryly. "It was awful."

"Green?" Alice popped her gum. "Narly."

Maggie bit back a smile. "To make matters worse, it was the week before my junior prom. My hair was more colorful than my gown."

Alice laughed and snapped the gum again, then after a warning look from Maggie, slipped it out of her mouth and tossed it in the trash. "I think I might dye mine back." She shrugged. "I don't know."

Maggie crossed her fingers but said easily, "It's your hair, your decision. But I'll never forget how happy I was to have my own boring black back." She handed the girl her apron. "Hang this up for me when you go back, would you?"

After Alice took it and started to move away, Maggie added quietly, "And Alice, I depend on you being here on time. If I can't, I'll have to find someone else."

Color crept up the girl's cheeks, and she lowered her eyes. "I'm sorry," she murmured. "I didn't know how...I mean, the other kids..." She slid her gaze to

Louise who was helping a customer, then shook her head. "It won't happen again."

Maggie nodded. "Good. We can talk more at the house later. I promised Dad and Jack I'd try out a couple of new cookie recipes. If they're exceptional, I'll bring some over."

After telling Louise she would talk to her later, Maggie headed back to the house. The phone was ringing as she stepped inside. She rushed to get it, catching it a moment before the answering machine.

"Hello," she murmured, working to catch her breath.

"Mrs. Adler?"

"Yes?"

"Congratulations! It's a girl."

"Pardon me?"

"This is Melanie Kane from Associated Charities.... We spoke about a year ago.... And I sent you a letter about your placement on our list." The woman paused. "You did receive our letter?"

"Well, yes. But—"

"You have a baby daughter. She's coming home the day after tomorrow. Congratulations!"

A baby daughter? Maggie stared blankly at the painting above the mantel. It depicted a summer garden in full bloom, and often over the past couple of years Maggie had thought of getting rid of it.

The woman, obviously used to shocked silences, rambled on. "I know you have a lot of preparations to make between now and then, so I won't keep you.

But I do look forward to seeing you and Mr. Adler Friday morning. We'll be there about ten.''

A moment later Maggie set the phone back in the cradle, her heart thumping almost painfully against the wall of her chest. She was a mother. She had a daughter. A baby.

She felt blindly for a chair, found one and sank onto it. She clasped her trembling hands in her lap. Could it be true? Could anyone be so cruel as to play a joke like this one?

She reached in her pocket and pulled out the envelope Royce had brought her. She ripped it open. All it said was that her and Royce's paperwork was in order and that their name was inching up the list.

Maggie pressed the letter to her chest, breathing hard. It was true. It wasn't a joke. Dear, God, she was going to be a mother.

Joy bloomed inside her. She smiled, then laughed. A daughter, the woman had said. Healthy, with ten fingers and ten toes. Big blue eyes and a cap of dark curls.

Maggie hugged herself, laughing again. She and Royce were parents.

Her smile faded. She looked back at the painting, her stomach crashing to her toes, her joy with it.

Royce. Oh, dear God. Royce.

What was she going to do?

Chapter Two

Maggie stood outside Sassy's, the cold wind pulling at her hair and coat, stinging her cheeks and hands. Hours had passed since the call from the adoption worker, and in that time she'd gone over and over what had happened, had asked herself the same questions again and again.

Each time the answers had been the same—without Royce, there would be no baby; without Royce her dream of becoming a mother would die.

Without Royce. Her eyes filled with tears and she stared at the restaurant's handsome brass-and-mahogany door. *How would she go on?*

She'd existed for eight and a half months without truly grasping what had happened, without really facing the fact that her marriage was over. And now, presented with the joy that could have been, this chance at a new life, the truth of her situation had hit her square in the chest.

She wiped at the moisture on her cheeks. She'd even wondered, crazily, in these past hours, if she couldn't win him back—beg him for another chance, find some way to make him believe there was a future for them.

But how could she convince him of something she wasn't sure she believed herself? She and Royce were nothing alike, from their preferences in food to their dreams of the future. What they had shared, what she'd so desperately loved had been an illusion only— a fiery storybook romance, complete with a handsome prince and a penniless but good-hearted maiden.

And even if all that weren't true—she couldn't love a man who had no room in his heart for children.

Maggie rummaged in her purse for a tissue. People on the busy French Quarter corner brushed by her; she felt their curious glances, knew she must appear a kook to them. But still she stood, rooted to the spot, too terrified to move, too filled with hope not to.

It was time to start her future. To do so, she needed her past.

How would Royce respond to her proposal? Her already frenetic heartbeat quickened at the thought, and she drew in a deep, shuddering breath. *Dear Lord, would she be able to convince him?*

She had to. It was her only chance.

Straightening her shoulders, she crossed the sidewalk and pushed through the door. Sassy's foyer was warm and softly lit. Still early for the dinner crowd, the restaurant echoed with preparatory sounds from the kitchen, conversation from idle waiters and the laughter of a group in the bar.

She glanced around, uncomfortable. The appointments, even here, were impeccable; the atmosphere a calculated combination of fun and sophistication. And as with everything associated with the Adlers, there was an elegance here, a rarefied wordliness that had always made her feel a bit of a country bumpkin.

"Maggie?"

Maggie recognized her sister-in-law Honoria's cultured voice and turned and faced her. The woman's meticulously shaped brows were arched ever so slightly in shock, and Maggie automatically reached up to smooth her own wild hair. Royce's family had always had a way of doing that to her, of making her question her appearance, doubt her choice of attire or meal or words.

"One for dinner?" Honoria asked coolly, arching her brows a bit more. "I don't remember seeing Ryan in the reservation book."

Maggie took a step back, surprised by the hostility in her sister-in-law's eyes and voice. Honoria had always been cool to her, but never unkind. She had disapproved of Royce's choice but, unlike her mother, had never attempted to break them up or to hurt her. Obviously that had changed.

Maggie clasped her hands together, her eyes brimming with tears. "I need to see Royce. Is he...here?"

For a moment it looked as if Honoria were going to say no, then without speaking she took Maggie's arm and ushered her out of the foyer and toward Royce's office. As they passed the bar Honoria ordered the bartender to bring a brandy.

Honoria didn't knock. Royce's office smelled as it always had, of leather and lemony polish. Seated at his desk, he looked up slowly, his obvious irritation at being disturbed giving way to shock. "My God, Maggie." He stood and came around the desk. "What's happened?"

She looked at Honoria, then up at him helplessly. She wanted to lean against him, wanted his strong arms to circle and support her. A hysterical laugh bubbled to her lips. What was it about her that always made her yearn for the impossible?

"You're trembling. Come." He put his arm around her and led her across to the big leather couch. "Sit." He pushed her gently into it, then swearing, turned to Honoria. "What's going on?"

The other woman shrugged. "I assure you, I haven't the faintest. She's your wife, after all. But I have ordered a brandy—ah, here it is now." She took the glass from the curious bartender, then, dismissing him, passed it to Royce. "I'll give you your...privacy now."

She started for the door, adding as she did, "The Richmond party will be here soon, and they'll expect to see you."

"I know what my obligations are," Royce snapped, squatting in front of Maggie with the drink. "Let me know when they arrive. Here," he said, forcing the glass into Maggie's hands. "It'll make you feel better."

Maggie thought about refusing, then took a sip. The fiery liquid slid down her throat, warming her. She curled her fingers tighter around the glass. "Royce... something's happened, and I...I need to talk to you. But I'm not sure how—" Her throat closed over the words again and she took another sip of the brandy.

"Does this have something to do with Alice? Has she gotten into some sort of—"

"No." Maggie shook her head vehemently. "Alice is doing great."

"Your mother or father, then? One of the kids?"

Maggie shook her head once more. "No...this..." She took a deep breath and met his eyes. "This has to do with...us."

"Us?" Royce repeated, sitting back on his heels.

"Yes. I..." She brushed a hand across her forehead, then swore silently as she saw it trembled. Taking another deep breath, she said, "Associated Charities called this afternoon."

He frowned. "The people who sent the letter?"

"Yes."

"And?"

"They have a baby for us, Royce," she said, her words spilling out in an excited rush. "A daughter."

Royce stared at her. Surely he had misunderstood, surely she hadn't said—

"A baby," Maggie repeated, catching his hands, not able to hold back a smile of wonder. "I can't believe it's true."

Royce jerked his hands from hers and stood, furious. He hadn't misunderstood. But he *had* underestimated her gall. "It seems you've forgotten something, Maggie. Like the fact we don't live together anymore. Like the fact we're getting a divorce."

She flinched. "How could I forget that, Royce? What do you take me for?"

"You tell me. You're the one who waltzed in here talking about 'our baby,' as if that made everything okay between us—as if now we could be one big, happy family."

"I didn't mean it that way," she whispered, pain at his words, his anger, slicing through her. This moment could have been so different, so wonderful, if only...

The time for "if onlys" was over. Straightening her shoulders, she stood and faced him. "And I didn't come here to fight with you."

He moved his gaze coldly over her. "No?"

"No." Maggie lowered her eyes to her hands, realizing then that she still clutched the brandy snifter. She carefully set it aside, then met his gaze once more. "I haven't come to fight. I've come to ask a . . . favor."

"A favor," he repeated, his mouth tightening with fury. "Nine months ago you asked me the favor of moving out of our home, now you want another?"

"I didn't ask you to move—" She caught the words and her own anger, her hurt. This wasn't about their past; it wasn't the time to argue over something that couldn't be changed. This was about the future, her future. She took a step toward him. "Hear me out, Royce. Please."

The look in her eyes tore at him and he swung away from her and crossed to the window. The traditional French Quarter courtyard beyond was illuminated by a single floodlight; the patio looked, at once, too bright and too shadowed. And unnaturally empty.

He took a deep, steadying breath, surprised by his own anger, attempting to get it in check. He'd thought his feelings for Maggie were tucked neatly away, had prided himself on his control, his civility. Where had this vehemence come from? And what did it say about his feelings?

"Royce...please."

"Okay," he murmured, not turning, not trusting himself to. "I'm listening."

Maggie clasped her hands together and wished he would look at her, although she wasn't sure it would make what she had to say any easier. In truth, the only thing that would make this easier was to once again wish for the impossible.

"We never filed for a legal separation," she said finally, softly. "We never started divorce proceedings. I didn't notify any of the adoption agencies we'd listed with of the...change in our marriage. As far as the world's concerned, we're still husband and wife."

"We are," he snapped, still not looking at her.

"I mean," she amended, her cheeks heating, "that to the world, we're still...happily married."

He did look at her then, narrowing his eyes. "So?"

"So..." She fought to keep her voice from faltering. "If you would move back in, if you would pretend to be—"

His bark of laughter cut her off. "You want me to move back in? Just like that? This is rich."

"No, not just like that," she corrected, crossing to him. She shook so badly, she folded her arms across her chest to steady herself. "It would be for appearances only, and only until the adoption's final. Amanda will be my baby. I promise you won't have any responsibility for—"

"You've already named her?"

Maggie stared at him, shocked to realize she had. "I...always liked the name and...I...always thought I'd name a daughter...Amanda."

"I see," he said quietly, dangerously. "And if we'd been able to have a child, and if it had been a girl, would I have had any say in her name? Or would you have gotten your way or...walked?" Even as he uttered the words he knew they were unfair, that he'd said them only to hurt her as she'd hurt him. But even the truth of that, even his own disappointment in himself, couldn't stop them from coming. "Or maybe I should say instead, gotten your way or made me walk."

Maggie blanched and swung away from him, blinking against tears. "If I had been able to conceive, if we'd had a child..." She shook her head, the tears choking her.

Pain curled through him, pain and futility. He reached out to touch her, to comfort and, without words, console them both. As he did, Honoria tapped on the door and he dropped his hand.

"Royce...Mrs. Richmond is here. She's asking for you."

Royce bit back a sound of frustration. "I'll be out in a moment."

"Go ahead," Maggie murmured, brushing at her cheeks, not wanting him to see her tears. "I'll wait."

Royce stared at her stiff back. He shook his head. "I don't think so, Maggie. Let's get this over with."

Like so much unpleasantness. There had been a time when he would have wanted her here, a time when he would have sneaked away at every opportunity and they would have necked on this big leather couch until they were both crazy with need and denial. The tears brimmed over again, slipping down her cheeks.

"Move back in with me," she said, her words choked. "Pretend to be the devoted and happy husband. I won't expect you to participate in any way— not with the baby or any other part of my life. It takes approximately seven months from the time the baby comes home for the adoption to become final. When it does, you can leave. No strings, Royce. No complications."

No strings? Royce thought, staring at her in disbelief. No complications? There were already so many of both, he would never be disentangled again.

He crossed to his desk and gazed down at the papers scattered across it. She hadn't thought of anyone but herself, her life, her needs. She certainly hadn't considered the fact she was using him—she needed a warm body, any husband would have done. Conveniently, she still had him.

He turned and faced her, shaking with anger. "So this is why you never filed for a divorce."

Maggie took a step back, stunned. "No! I never thought something like this could happen. I didn't plan it."

"No? Well even if you hadn't, the outcome would have been the same. Now, if there's nothing else, I have a restaurant to run."

"Royce! Please!" Maggie grabbed his hands in desperation. "Do you remember the day I came home from the doctor—the first one who told me I'd never have children?"

Royce gazed at her, dragged his thoughts back to that day, that time. Her tears, her desolation, had torn at him. As had his own terrible feeling of helplessness.

And guilt. Because he hadn't felt the same as she. He still didn't.

"How could I forget?" he murmured, his voice thick.

"And the day I had my hysterectomy?"

"Yes."

"I can't have children, Royce. Not ever. You lived through that time with me, but still you can't imagine what it felt like. How it feels now. To want something so badly, yet have it be so far out of reach—something that's supposed to be guaranteed to me because of my sex. All women can make babies, everybody knows that. That's what I'd always believed. But it's not true. Some of us...can't.''

Royce lowered his eyes to their joined hands. Hers seemed so small and fragile in his. He lifted his gaze back to her face.

She tightened her fingers. "If you choose to, you can father a dozen children someday. This is my only chance, Royce.''

"Maggie, I...''

Tears filled her eyes and slid down her cheeks. "I want to be a mother, Royce. It's all I've ever really wanted. From the day my own mother deserted me.''

She clasped his hands tighter, absorbing their warmth and strength, feeling comforted even though it was she who clung to him. "The Ryans loved me— they took me in and cared for me—but they weren't mine...we didn't belong to each other. I've never had anything that was just mine.''

"I was yours, Maggie.''

"It's not the same." She shook her head. "How can I make you see the difference?''

"You can't," he murmured, slipping his hands from hers. "Obviously. We tried this before. I always understood your wanting a child, Maggie—just not your all-encompassing *need* for one. I wish I could, though. Maybe then we...'' He shook his head and let the thought trail off. "All I can see, all I can understand, is that you were never wholly mine . . . and I was never enough.''

''This isn't about us.''

''Isn't it?'' He laughed, the sound dry and aching even to his own ears. ''You ask me to live with you again in a mockery of what we once shared, and you tell me this isn't about us?''

''This is about me.'' She pressed a hand to her chest for emphasis. ''You should be able to understand that. After all, wasn't that one of our problems? When it came to children, wasn't it always only about me?''

''That's not fair, Maggie. I loved you enough to try. I wanted you to be happy. More than anything . . . I wanted you to be happy.''

''Make me happy now.'' He turned away from her, and she took a step toward him, her hand stretched out in supplication. ''Please, Royce. Please do this for me.''

''Is what you're proposing honest?'' he asked quietly. ''Is it moral?''

She sucked in a sharp breath, hating herself in so many small ways. Crossing to him, she touched his back with trembling fingertips. He flinched, and she bit back a sound of pain. ''No, it's not. But no child will be more loved. Isn't that what it's supposed to be all about? Providing a good home, a loving family?''

She touched him again, wishes and regrets tumbling through her, the feelings of the past mixing with those of the present. ''Maybe Amanda won't have a traditional family, with a mother and a father, but she'll have lots of doting aunts and uncles and cousins. And I'll be a good mother, Royce. I have so much love to give . . . I have such a need to give it."

Aching, Royce squeezed his eyes shut. What she said was true, she would be a wonderful, loving mother. And the Ryans. . . . Well that brood would be a storybook kind of extended family.

Torn, he opened his eyes and looked at her. Her face was ravaged by tears and . . . hope. Her lips trembled and her eyes glimmered with yet more tears. Two parents didn't ensure a happy childhood or an abundance of love—he knew that firsthand. And his doubts about their becoming parents had never had anything to do with Maggie's ability to give, only his own inability.

Maybe this was the right thing to do. Maybe—

Honoria rapped on the office door. "Royce, for God's sake . . . the Richmonds!"

"All right, I'm co—"

"Please," Maggie whispered hoarsely, lacing their fingers, tightening them as he tried to move away from her. If he left her now, she would lose. She had no doubts about that fact. "Please, Royce."

"I don't know." He eased his hand from hers and started toward the door. "I need time to think about this."

At the sound of her sob, he stopped and looked back at her. She stood ramrod-straight, save for the effort of holding back her sobs. She seemed so small and lost standing there. So beaten.

Something twisted in his chest and he swore. Even though it was over between them, even though he knew this was the wrong thing to do, he could refuse her nothing. Right or wrong, just as when they'd lived together.

"All right, Maggie," he said. "No strings, no responsibilities. When the adoption's final, I walk."

Maggie opened her mouth to thank him, but he was already gone. Shaking, she sank onto the couch. She'd won the battle but somehow lost the war. For even though her dream of motherhood was coming true, she felt as if she had lost something just as precious.

She dropped her head into her hands and wept.

Chapter Three

What had he gotten himself into?

Royce paused outside the gate and stared up at the house he had once shared with Maggie. That he would share with her again, he corrected himself, frowning. Right or wrong, uncomfortable or not, he'd committed himself. For the next seven or so months, he and Maggie would live together as husband and wife.

With some important differences. It was those that worried him most. How would it feel to live with Maggie and not be able to touch her? To exist under the same roof, but with separate bedrooms? He thought of the four-poster bed they had shared and of Maggie in it, her dark hair fanned across the pillow, her eyes sultry with wanting.

The bedroom was the one place he and Maggie had always been in accord.

Shoving thoughts of big, soft mattresses and even softer caresses aside, Royce opened the gate and started slowly up the walk. Nothing about the house or grounds had changed, although the inside, he knew, would be different than he remembered. He'd taken his art and the antiques that had been passed to him by his maternal grandmother, as well as his personal mementos and clothing. Everything else he'd left. He had wanted nothing that they'd bought together.

Including the house. An ache in his chest, he climbed the steps to the veranda. There, he stopped and turned back to the view of Lake Pontchartrain, silver in the morning light. They'd chosen this house over others along the lake in Old Mandeville because of the very southernness of it—from this wide, graceful veranda, to the half dozen live oaks dripping with Spanish moss, to the long shell drive and wrought-iron fence circling the deep front yard.

"We'll grow old together in this house," Maggie had said, laughing up at him. "We'll sit in rocking chairs, sip iced teas and watch our grandchildren play."

He'd laughed with her, teasing about how she might look in forty years. Then he had kissed her, long and hard, right there in front of God, the neighbors and anyone else who happened to walk by.

That had been the day they moved in, the renovations to the one-hundred-and-ten-year-old structure finally complete. That had been before Maggie discovered she couldn't have children, before it had all started to crumble around them.

Less than a year later he had moved out.

"You're here."

Royce turned slowly toward the door and Maggie, wondering what she would see in his expression. In hers he saw excitement and nerves...and sadness. He understood the last most of all. "Yes."

"Come in."

He hoisted his bags and followed her inside. As he'd known there would be, there were changes. She'd moved the furniture in the main parlor, substituting brightly colored floor pillows for the antiques he'd taken. The walls were a peachy cream hue now instead of the cool beige they'd first chosen. This year's Jazz Festival poster hung above the mantel, replacing the family portrait he'd taken with him; she'd arranged various green plants strategically around the room, filling empty spaces and corners.

"It's not as elegant," she murmured, clasping her hands together. "But I spend a lot of time in this room and this...suits me."

As he hadn't.

Her words—the thought—stung, even though they shouldn't have. He looked at her, suddenly and unreasonably angry. But as he did, his anger evaporated. She wore navy trousers and a matching cardigan. Her blouse was white and dressy; she'd made an attempt to tame her mane of black waves by French-braiding it.

And she was terrified. He saw it in the way she fidgeted, in the slightly haunted look in her big, dark eyes, in the rapid rise and fall of her chest. Assurances sprang to his lips; he swallowed them.

"Perhaps I should get rid of these," he said instead, roughly. "It wouldn't look good to have suitcases cluttering up the hallway."

"Yes." She folded her arms across her chest, then dropped them to her sides. "You're right, of course. I'll take you up."

He followed her up the wide staircase, the sense of déjà vu warring with one of displacement. He'd belonged, now he didn't; she'd been his, now she wasn't.

"I put you in the guest room with the sitting room attached," she said. "I thought you might like some...privacy."

"Thank you."

"The nursery," she continued breathlessly, "is complete. Or maybe I should say ready instead of complete. We couldn't paint, because of the fumes. And wallpaper is such a bear to put up. We just didn't have the time to fight with it." She laughed, the sound more about nerves than amusement. "Even so, we worked around the clock. I don't know what I would have done without my sisters and brothers. And Alice, of course."

"Of course," he repeated stiffly. He couldn't blame the girl for him and Maggie splitting up; he shouldn't be angry with her. Yet Alice had been the final straw, the catalyst for Maggie's ultimatum and his moving out.

She lived here now. And he didn't.

"I never would have guessed," she continued, moving down the hallway, "there would be so much to buy, so much one baby would need—bottles and diapers and formula and receiving blankets and..." She stopped in front of the guest-room door and let out an unsteady breath. "I just hope I haven't forgotten anything."

"It's going to be all right, Maggie." The words were out before he could stop them, before he even knew they were there.

She met his eyes, her own a bit glassy. "You think so?"

"I wouldn't have said it if I hadn't meant it."

She touched his arm in thanks, just once and lightly; he felt her fingers like a brand. Sucking in a sharp breath he turned away quickly, not wanting her to see how strongly her innocent gesture had affected him.

He scowled. Agreeing to this had been a mistake. They couldn't go back; there was no future for them. And the present, with its mixture of memories, cynicism and temptation, was hell.

"Royce?"

Her voice quivered—just a bit, just enough to tear at him. Her emotionalism had always affected him this way, and he steeled himself against the urge to pull her into his arms to comfort and protect her.

What she wanted from him, he reminded himself, had nothing to do with wanting him.

"If you'll excuse me, Maggie. I'll unpack."

She dropped her hand and stepped back, stung. "The adoption worker should be here with Amanda in thirty minutes. Would you like me to—"

"I'll be down."

She took another step, holding on to her pride. "Fine. I'll see you then."

Without another word he crossed into his bedroom and shut the door behind him. For long moments Maggie stared at the closed door. What was she doing? He'd given her one little reassurance and she'd reacted like a love-starved puppy.

The image made her cringe, and she turned away from the door. He'd made his feelings abundantly clear; there would be no agonizing for Royce. No annoying little emotions getting in the way of clear thinking. Oh, no, she thought, with a trace of bitterness, Royce would keep it all in perspective. He always had.

She thought of the way he'd jerked away from her touch, and her cheeks burned.

It didn't hurt, Maggie told herself almost fiercely. She could keep all this in perspective just as well as he. She curled her fingers into her palms. She wouldn't allow herself to forget why he was here or what had transpired between them. She wouldn't allow him to hurt her again. It was as simple as that.

Simple? Maggie almost laughed. He'd stepped through the front door and the house had immediately become theirs again, instead of hers. He'd only had to move across the threshold and the house had seemed fuller, more alive. He'd only had to murmur one soft word and she'd melted.

Maggie moved slowly back down the hall, fighting the urge to give in to tears. Simple? she thought again. How could anything be simple—she still loved him.

She shook her head, furious with herself for the thought. Today was the first day of the rest of her life. A cliché, but true. Today her dream of becoming a mother would become a reality; today she would begin to put the past behind her. It would hurt. But pain was a part of life.

Just as joy was.

Maggie stopped in the nursery doorway, her lips lifting in an automatic smile. White crib, changing table and dresser. A big old-fashioned rocker waiting in the corner. Drawers filled with soft flannel blankets and even softer little outfits.

She stepped into the room, which two days ago had been the master bedroom's sitting room. She crossed to the crib, running her hand along its slats, then smoothing the frilly pastel comforter and plumping the tiny pillow in its matching pillowcase. A fat, fluffy cinnamon bear guarded one corner of the crib, a big, soft rabbit another. Above the crib, a colorful clown mobile swayed.

She tapped one of the clowns, smiling again. Alice had bought both the bear and rabbit, Maggie's mom and dad had brought the mobile the night before. Her family had been great. They'd been surprised and thrilled by her news; everyone had pitched in and helped with the nursery and the shopping, even offering their time at the coffeehouse until she was ready to go back to work.

Her smile faltered, then faded. She'd told everyone but Louise that she and Royce were going to try to make a go of it again—because they loved each other and because of the baby. She had believed the fib would be easier, because she wouldn't have to try to explain to everyone what she was doing and why, or defend her decision to those who thought it a mistake. Her father would never have understood the truth; her mother would have worried, and her brother Jack would have insisted on a heart-to-heart talk with Royce.

But now guilt gnawed at her. She'd never lied to her family before; she didn't like keeping secrets. And she suspected her "easy way out" had complicated an already hopelessly tangled situation. Her sisters were asking why they hadn't seen Royce; her dad was celebrating the fact that the threat of divorce no longer hung over the good Ryan name, and her mother had been too quiet, as if she suspected something closer to the truth and was hurt by Maggie's deception.

The last bothered her most. Eileen Ryan had taken her in when she had more than any one woman should be asked to handle already, and she'd opened her arms and heart and had never looked back.

Maggie trailed her fingers across the pastel-colored comforter. Louise had stuck by her, although she'd had serious doubts about her decision. And who could blame Louise for those doubts? Her decision had been the act of a desperate woman, and decisions made in desperation were often foolhardy.

"It's almost time," Alice said from the doorway.

Maggie turned and smiled at her. "I know. But thanks anyway."

Alice shifted her weight from one foot to the other. "Louise is here. She brought some stuff for us to eat. She's in the kitchen putting it away."

"I guess I should go down then."

Alice clasped her hands awkwardly in front of her. "Everything looks real pretty, Maggie. Amanda's a lucky little girl."

Tears sprang to Maggie's eyes. No other words could have made her feel as good. "You really think so?"

"Yeah."

Alice's eyes brimmed, too, and Maggie crossed to her and hugged her. The girl stiffened, then relaxed and returned the hug, almost clinging to her.

"Have I told you lately how great you are?" Maggie whispered, emotion choking the words.

Alice started to pull away, but Maggie stopped her, meeting her gaze evenly. "You are, you know. And don't let anyone tell you differently."

Seeing the girl's discomfort, Maggie released her. If she pushed too hard or too fast, Alice would run. And all the good she'd accomplished would be lost. "You dyed your hair back," she said lightly. "I'm glad."

"Me, too." The girl touched it self-consciously. "It was a dumb thing to do."

Maggie tipped her head. "I like the new length, though. It shows off your great cheekbones."

Alice just looked away, and Maggie ached for her. "We all make mistakes, Alice," she said softly. "It's part of being human."

Her shoulders slumped, and she stubbed her toe into the carpet. "I guess."

"It's true." Maggie drew her eyebrows together. "And don't you dare think it!"

Alice angled a glance up at her. "What?"

"That you do more dumb things than other people. Because it's not true, Alice. You're very bright."

She started to shake her head. "Nobody's ever—"

"That's *their* problem," Maggie said quietly. "Not yours."

Alice stared at her for a moment, then smiled shyly. "For real?"

That such an intelligent and lovely young woman could think so little of herself was a sin. Sometimes it made her so angry she wanted to find Alice's parents and shake them.

Like now. She smiled instead. "Yeah, for real."

Alice beamed. "I did get a B-plus on my last math quiz. Mrs. Wilkes said if I kept it up..."

The doorbell rang and Maggie jumped. "Oh, my God, Alice, it's them." She held a trembling hand to her chest and took a deep breath. "I feel like I'm going to faint or something."

"You'd better not," Louise said from the hallway behind her. "You have a baby to take care of."

Maggie whirled around, laughing nervously. "Do I look all right? I mean, do I look like a mother?"

Louise shook her head, amused. "No. In four weeks you'll look like a mother. Now you look like someone who's about to wet her pants." The bell sounded again and Louise jerked her thumb in the direction of the stairs. "Come on, Mommy."

Maggie followed her, stopping in the doorway as she remembered Alice. She swung back around. "Oh, Alice, I'm sorry! Can we finish this talk another time?"

"Sure." Alice folded her arms around herself. "No problem."

"Thanks." Maggie hesitated a moment, torn by the expression in Alice's eyes. "Are you coming?"

Alice shook her head. "I've got some... homework."

Maggie hesitated a moment more, and Louise tugged at her arm. Promising herself she would find a minute for Alice later, Maggie turned and headed downstairs.

Royce was right behind her. They reached the door together. Instinctively, she reached for his hand, then realizing what she was doing, moved to grasp the doorknob instead. Royce beat her to it and he swung the door open.

It hadn't been a joke or a dream, Maggie thought dizzily. Melanie Kane from Associated Charities stood on the other side of the threshold, a bundle in pink blankets nestled in her arms.

Maggie lowered her gaze, her smile freezing, her mind emptying of everything but the fact that, as of this moment, she was a mother. She sucked in a deep breath and stared at the infant, stunned by the feelings barreling through her. If she had wondered whether she would feel awkward about Amanda, if she had worried she wouldn't love her, she'd wasted both time and energy. She felt so much love, she wondered if her heart could possibly hold it all.

Mutely, she held out her arms and the woman placed Amanda in them, murmuring something about supporting the head. Maggie nodded, not able to tear her eyes away from Amanda long enough to even acknowledge that the woman had spoken.

This was her baby. Her daughter.

Maggie brushed her lips across Amanda's forehead. The infant smelled of baby powder and formula; her skin was softer, smoother than anything she'd ever touched before. And she was beautiful. Gorgeous. Light seemed to radiate from her. Lips curving into a smile, Maggie lifted her eyes to Royce's. He, too, stared at Amanda, his expression stunned.

"May I come in?"

Maggie looked at the adoption worker, realizing she had forgotten all about her. Royce stepped smoothly in. "Of course. And I apologize for our lack of manners."

The woman waved his apology aside, laughing. "I'm used to this. And truthfully, cold wind or not, it's the best part of the job. Congratulations, again."

"Thank you," Maggie murmured, cuddling Amanda closer to her chest. "I can't tell you how happy and excited I am, or how much this means to me."

"And what about you, Mr. Adler?" Maggie held her breath as a smiling Melanie Kane turned to him. "You seem stunned."

"Stunned is not quite the word I'd choose," Royce said softly. "But it will do."

Maggie's heart plummeted to her knees, but the woman laughed. "I know. Most couples have nine months to become accustomed to the idea of parenthood. It's all so sudden this way. Not enough time even to get your bearings."

"You could say that again." Royce closed the door behind them. "Can I offer you some refreshment, Ms. Kane?"

She refused, insisted they call her Melanie, then began going over how and what to feed Amanda and what to expect out of her in the coming weeks. She had a book on parenting for them, some formula samples and a half dozen disposable diapers. She laughed and called it their "parent pack," then asked to see the house and nursery.

Maggie was glad to let Royce lead the tour and introduce her to Louise.

During it all he was absolutely charming. The loving husband, he touched her elbow now and again, her shoulder, her hair. Each time he did, she fought the urge to lean into him, fought the ache of wanting and regret.

But he didn't touch Amanda, not once.

She shouldn't have been surprised by that; it shouldn't have hurt. They had a deal, after all. But it did hurt, unreasonably and deeply.

"Well, that's about it," Melanie said as they descended the staircase. "Remember, feed her on demand—and believe me, you'll know when she's hungry. You'll be surprised, at first, to see how much and how often she eats. Expect to have to feed her every two hours for the next few months." They reached the foyer and crossed to the front door. "I have some papers for you to sign, and once that's done I'll leave you alone to enjoy your daughter."

They took care of the paperwork, then Royce let her out and watched as she walked to her car. When she'd driven off, he crossed to the closet and took out his topcoat. "She's all yours, Maggie." He shrugged into the coat. "Don't expect me for dinner."

He let himself out and started across the lawn to the shell drive. Sucking in a deep breath of the cold air, he jammed his hands into his coat pockets.

"Royce!" Louise called, racing across the veranda after him. "Wait!"

He wanted to keep going. He stopped and turned back toward her instead.

"Why did you do that?" she demanded, stopping in front of him, her breath making little puffs of steam in the cold, damp air. "How could you do that?"

He lifted his eyebrows coolly. "Do what, Louise?"

"Walk out like that! She's devastated."

Royce made a sound of impatience. "You're over-reacting. Maggie and I have a deal. She under-stands—"

"We're talking about emotions here—not about some cold-blooded deal."

"What would you have me do?" he asked stiffly. "Stay and play with the baby? Try feeding her or changing a diaper?" He shoved his clenched hands deeper into his topcoat's pockets. "She's not mine, Louise. Maggie made it clear what my role is here. I'm a piece of meat. A convenience. I don't take part in Amanda's life... or Maggie's. After the adoption's final, the marriage will be over, once and for all." He shook his head, frustrated. "But I'm sure you know all that."

"Royce...I didn't..." Louise took a step back, her expression stunned. "I mean, how do you feel-about—"

"Feel?" He laughed tightly. "What do feelings have to do with this? This is a favor. I made a deal with my...wife." He turned away from her, suddenly cold. "I have to go to work, Louise. Let's *not* continue this talk another time."

She didn't try to stop him, but as he backed his car out of the drive he saw that she hadn't moved, that she still stared at him. He looked from her to the house. Maggie stood in the window watching him leave, Amanda cradled in her arms.

He swore. He *wasn't* supposed to feel anything. Not for Amanda. Not for Maggie. But he hadn't expected the baby to be quite so tiny. So fragile-looking.

Dammit. What had happened to the sturdy cherub he'd expected?

And Maggie—he hadn't expected her to be so beautiful with Amanda in her arms; he hadn't been prepared for the joy that emanated from her.

A lump formed in his throat and he shoved the car into first gear. And he hadn't expected to feel so alienated by that joy.

Depressing the accelerator, he flew out of the driveway and toward the causeway.

Amanda's cry came at 2:00 a.m. Maggie stumbled out of bed, searching blindly for the robe she'd meant to lay out but realized now that she had forgotten.

"I'm coming, sweetheart," she murmured, pushing the hair out of her eyes. "Just a minute, baby."

Deciding to forget the robe, she raced down the stairs and into the kitchen, stubbing her toe on an out-of-place chair. She flipped on the overhead light, then made a sound of pain. She covered her eyes. Night-lights, she thought. She had to put more night-lights on the list.

She opened the refrigerator. She hadn't forgotten to make bottles. Thank God. She loosened the cap of one and stuck it in the microwave, just the way Louise had showed her, just the way she had been doing all afternoon. Shivering, she stared at the timer and bounced from one foot to the other. Slippers, she thought. And rugs. Thick, warm, woolly rugs.

The buzzer rang; she took the bottle from the oven, tightened the cap and tested a drop on her wrist.

"Ow!" Tears sprang to her eyes and she brought her wrist to her mouth. Dammit. She pushed the hair out of her eyes. What had she done wrong?

Amanda's wails increased in volume and Maggie's disorientation gave way to panic. She pulled another bottle from the fridge, repeated the whole procedure, then hit the stairs running—only tripping on the second and sixth steps.

She raced into the nursery. "Here I am, sweetheart," she crooned breathlessly. "Mommy's here." Maggie gathered the still-wailing Amanda into her arms and carried her to the rocker. The infant's body was rigid with tension, and when she found the nipple she made a sound almost primal in its relief.

Maggie held her, spellbound. Amanda nestled against her chest, greedily sucking, making smacking noises and small mewls of pleasure. And as the formula began to fill her, her muscles relaxed, her body softened and eased against Maggie's.

It was as if she'd been starving, Maggie thought wonderingly. She lightly stroked Amanda's dark curls and the infant made a soft, gurgling sound. Maggie's eyes filled with tears, a feeling of oneness, a protectiveness such as she'd never known, washing over her.

She drew in a deep breath, her chest aching with the effort. If only she could nourish Amanda from her own body. She'd never thought much about breast-feeding, had even wondered, back before she'd known to wonder such things was a waste of her time, if she would want to do it. Now, her heart hurt with the want.

Maggie loosened her gown, easing the buttons through the holes without disturbing Amanda's eating. The fabric slid down, off her left shoulder and over her chest until Amanda's velvety little head was pressed against her naked breast.

Maggie drew a deep, shuddering breath. She felt warm and . . . whole.

And wholly female.

A tear slipped down her cheek. Another followed. This was what it was to be essential, completely needed. This was what had always eluded her before.

She lifted her head. Royce stood just outside the doorway, still as stone, his eyes fixed on them. Their gazes met. Her heart stopped, then started again with a vengeance. In the minimal light, his face was bathed in shadow; she sensed rather than saw his expression.

Heat bloomed inside her—a different kind of warmth than that of a moment ago, but equally female. Equally intoxicating. Her nipples tightened; her mouth grew dry. She parted her lips to speak, but no sound came out.

Still he stood. Still their gazes locked. Heat became moisture; each second became an agony. Then without speaking, he turned and walked away.

She made a sound then, whether of relief or pain she didn't know. Her heart raced; her breath came in short, quick bursts. Amanda stirred, whimpering in protest, and Maggie forced herself to relax, forced herself to breathe evenly.

A lethargy, the aftereffect of unrelieved desire, stole over her body. Her limbs became heavy even as her mind whirled. She lifted Amanda to her shoulder, rubbed her back and rocked. Moments became minutes, minutes grouped together into lumps of time passing.

And as it seemed she'd done so often in her life, Maggie stared at the empty doorway and wondered what she'd done wrong.

Chapter Four

Amanda woke again at four, then at six and eight; the days flowed one into the next, until two weeks had passed. And Maggie flowed with them, in a mixture of wonder and exhaustion.

But even exhaustion and the miracle of Amanda hadn't dimmed her memory of those moments when she and Royce had stared at each other, or of the heat that had blossomed inside her.

And just as her memory of that night hadn't dimmed, neither had her confusion over it. As the days passed, she'd alternated between aching to see him and praying she wouldn't.

Maggie propped her chin on her fist and gazed into the smoldering fire. The "wouldn'ts" had won. Which was just as well, she told herself for the billionth time. Really it was. Relationships ended, people ended them. If her past had taught her anything, it was that. She also knew from that same painful past, that emotions played traitor, often lagging behind and denying reality.

Maybe she would love Royce forever, or maybe, as it had been with her mother, one day she would wake up and realize she was free. But whatever the outcome to her heart, it was over between them. She had to remember that. She had her own life, her own future before her.

Her future. She shifted her gaze from the hearth to Amanda, asleep on a quilt beside her. Smiling softly, Maggie tucked the blanket a little closer around her. She'd thought herself so smart in bringing Amanda down here to play, had thought it would be nice and cozy in front of the fire.

And it would have been, if she could have gotten the silly thing to light. She rubbed her chilled hands together.

Maggie sighed. More than a change of pace from the nursery, she'd wanted the company of a cheerful fire. The house had seemed so quiet all day, so empty; the approaching evening had stretched endlessly before her. She shook her head, an annoying little ache in her chest. She must have looked forward to the day with her family more than she'd thought.

"Hello, Maggie."

Maggie jumped at Royce's softly spoken words. Hand to her throat, she swiveled around to look at him. As he had the other night, he stood in the doorway watching her. Only this time she could read his expression very well, and the aloofness there made a mockery of her own turbulent emotions.

"I didn't hear you come in," she said, her words sounding lame even to her own ears.

"And I didn't expect you to be home." He stepped into the room, loosening his tie. "The Thanksgiving extravaganza must have ended early this year."

"I didn't go." Maggie fiddled with the end of her long braid. "Colin and Nicky have colds, and Jonathan's just getting over the flu. I didn't want to chance Amanda catching anything."

"Once upon a time you said you'd never miss one."

He had wanted to go to Aspen that year. He'd wanted to teach her to snow ski. Aching at the happy memory, she murmured, "That was before Amanda."

"It was before a lot of things, wasn't it? It seems a lifetime ago now."

A lifetime ago—when he still loved her. Tears sprang to her eyes, and she turned back to the hearth.

Behind her, she heard him move farther into the room and set down his bag of take-out. "You made the fire yourself?"

"If you can call it that." She cleared her throat. "It doesn't seem to want to start."

"Allow me." He crossed to the fireplace and squatted down in front of it, adding more wood, restacking what was already there.

Maggie drew her knees to her chest and watched him work, his movements achingly familiar. He had a strong profile; it had been one of the things that had attracted her to him. His was a perfect nose, almost too straight for a man's. It was the kind of nose people paid big bucks for, the kind that made a face. Like so many other things in his life, Royce had gotten his for free.

She moved her gaze a bit lower. He had a great mouth, as well. A sensual mouth—chiseled, but not hard; demanding, but never ungenerous. She remembered exactly how it had felt on hers—the first time and the last.

And his smile...his smile had had the ability to steal her breath. She rested her chin on her drawn-up knees, a sadness stealing over her. She squeezed her eyes shut for a moment and pictured his smile as it had been so often. Wickedly sexy, tinged with male arrogance, he'd used it to woo her into bed the first time, had coaxed her time and again out of anger and into his arms.

Until the end, when she'd seen that smile so rarely, when she'd been too devastated by hurt to be coaxed, even if he had tried.

She caught her bottom lip between her teeth. Tonight he looked tired. The lines in his face seemed more deeply cut, his eyes shadowed. Even after everything that had happened, she longed to smooth away the lines with gentle fingers, to replace fatigue and frustration with a sleepy satisfaction.

"Rough day?" she asked softly, before she thought not to. The question was a wife's, the kind of wife she used to be. Having uttered it made her feel exposed and vulnerable.

Royce looked over his shoulder at her, meeting her eyes. In his she saw something other than indifference, something softer than anger, something intimate that stirred. A moment later it was gone.

He turned back to the fire. "Just a day." He struck a match and put it to the kindling. The flame caught and spread until the kindling was consumed.

"That should do it." He stood and brushed off his hands.

He hadn't looked at Amanda, not once. Even though it shouldn't, his disinterest hurt. "Thanks." Maggie folded her own hands in her lap, disturbed to realize they trembled. "I thought I was going to have to move Amanda back upstairs."

"Well...I guess I'll leave you to it." He moved back across the room to his bag of take-out, picked it up, then paused and turned back to her. "Have you eaten?"

She turned slowly, her heart thundering in her chest. She called herself a fool. "A sandwich at noon."

"Would you like to join me?"

"Oh...thanks. But I don't—"

"I have enough for four. It's Chinese."

She swallowed and lowered her eyes. Aching to say yes, she said, "I think I'll pass."

"Suit yourself." He crossed to the doorway, then stopped and swung back around. "No, Maggie. You're hungry, you're too exhausted to cook and you look like you might keel over any second. You're going to eat."

"Excuse me?" She looked at him in astonishment. He couldn't have just ordered her to eat. But he had. She jerked her chin up, angry heat stinging her cheeks. "I'm a big girl, Royce, and can fend for myself. I won't starve. Or keel over. Now, why don't you go eat your blasted—"

She bit the words off and glared at him. He looked for all the world like he wanted to laugh! "I don't know what I said that was so funny," she snapped. "But let me assure you—"

He held up his hands, take-out bag and all. "Poor word choice, Mags. I apologize if I offended you." His expression softened. "Let me rephrase my invitation. I'd be happy if you'd join me for dinner. The company would be nice."

He punctuated his words with a brilliant smile, and Maggie's indignation melted. She sank back against the huge floor pillows. He played her like a drum—and they both knew it. Nothing had changed.

"I guess I do need to eat," she said, knowing she sounded ungracious but not caring one bit.

His lips curved again, this time in satisfaction. "Good, I'll be right back."

He returned a moment later with everything they would need for their meal, including a bottle of red wine and two glasses. He poured her one.

Maggie accepted the glass, taking care so their fingers wouldn't brush. They did, anyway, and warmth flooded her face. She met his eyes, the memory of the other night filling her head. As it also filled his—she could see it in the heat of his gaze, feel it in the sudden and electric tension between them.

She dragged her gaze from his, ostensibly to check on Amanda. She fussed with the infant's quilt, lightly ran her fingers through the downy curls, then pressed them to her forehead to check her temperature. Amanda didn't stir at the caress, didn't even seem to breathe.

"Does she always sleep so deeply?"

Maggie looked back up at Royce, surprised to see him staring at Amanda. She smiled. "Yes. Sometimes, I have to touch her just to make sure she's still alive."

Royce brushed his index finger ever so softly against the baby's cheek. At the touch, the infant turned her head toward his finger and without even opening her eyes, started making sucking motions and sounds.

He snatched his hand back. "She must be hungry."

Maggie laughed, unreasonably pleased. "No, that's just a rooting reflex. It helps a newborn find its mother's nipple." She touched the baby's cheek again, and again Amanda started to suck. "You'll eat anytime, won't you baby," she cooed. "Mommy's little piggy. Maybe I better get you a bottle now and save us both your crying."

Maggie pressed a light kiss to the top of her head, then looked back up at Royce. "I'll be right back, don't let her go anywhere."

Don't let her go anywhere? Royce thought, frowning as he watched Maggie leave the room. Where would she go?

He turned back to the fire and pressed the heels of his hands to his eyes. Inviting Maggie to eat with him hadn't been the smartest thing he'd ever done, that he'd argued her into accepting had been sheer stupidity. What the hell had he been thinking?

Of the shadows under her eyes, he acknowledged, dropping his head back against the propped-up pillows. Of the way he'd found her, sitting alone and perfectly still in the fading light of the day and the fire, her hair a dark canopy against the cream of her sweater and the even whiter white of her skin.

Royce closed his eyes and the image of black hair against white, white skin filled his head. He swallowed against the dryness in his throat. He hadn't been able to put the night he stumbled upon her feeding Amanda out of his mind. He'd never seen her so beautiful. Even now he could picture her, the curve of her naked shoulder, golden in the glow of the nightlight, Amanda's small, dark head pressed against the swell of Maggie's breast, Maggie's black hair streaming down her back, over her shoulders.

There'd been something earthy and erotic and... right about the way she'd looked.

Arousal had punched him in the gut. Arousal and emotion.

Even though the arousal clung to him still, invading both his sleep and waking hours, it had been the emotion that had unnerved him—pure, unadulterated and totally befuddling.

Royce frowned. He wasn't accustomed to feeling so much. Or so keenly.

He turned his gaze back to the infant. Despite his vow to keep his distance from both Maggie and her baby, he'd found himself drawn to them. To Maggie, with thoughts of her in his arms, with remembrances of how it had been, and with needs—raw and physical and biting.

But oddly, and with great discomfiture, he'd been drawn to Amanda, as well. When he left in the morning and returned at night, he always peeked in the nursery—never stepped inside—but always peeked in to see if she was there and if all was well. He found himself listening for her cries in the night, not just being awakened by them, but listening for them as an anxious new parent might.

Which was ridiculous, of course.

Curiosity, he told himself, scowling. He'd never been around an infant before and, like anything foreign, Maggie's baby was a curiosity. He trailed his gaze over her relaxed form. That was why he wondered at the way her hands were always curled into fists, why he marveled at her ability to sleep so soundly and cry so loudly.

Sure.

Reaching down, he quickly and ever so lightly touched one of her fists with his forefinger. Her skin was incredibly soft. Smoother than any surface he'd ever known and almost translucent.

Amazing that we all begin this way, he thought, touching her hand again. So new and perfect. She stirred, spreading her fingers for a second before curling them once again into a fist.

A lump formed in his throat. He swallowed past it and eased both his hand and gaze away just as Maggie came back into the room.

After exchanging a few words, they filled their plates and began to eat. Silence stretched between them. Maggie sneaked a glance at Royce, then looked away. He seemed different than before she'd left the room—quieter, more withdrawn.

She pushed the food around her plate. It had been so long since they'd shared a meal—or anything else—she had no idea what to say. He probably felt as awkward about this as she did, although he would never admit it.

She took a bite of food. It almost stuck in her throat. She took a sip of wine, then unable to stand the silence another second, she murmured, "Everything's delicious."

"I'm glad you like it."

"Do you still go to that place on Poydras St—"

"They closed several months back."

"Oh . . . too bad."

He shrugged. "It's a tough market right now. With so many new restaurants opening, even good places can go down."

"Everything's okay at Sass—"

"Sassy's is doing great."

Silence fell between them again. Again she broke it. "So, what are you doing home tonight?"

He took a swallow of his wine, then stared into the burgundy-colored liquid for a moment before answering. "Mom and Dad are in Palm Springs. Honoria's handling Sassy's. You know holidays aren't a big deal in my family."

She did know. Maggie lowered her eyes to Amanda. It had been an area of discord between them—family had meant everything to her and almost nothing to him. Many of their problems had sprung from that one difference.

"How about Alice?" he asked suddenly. "Is she upstairs?"

"No." Maggie gave up all pretense of eating and set down her fork. "She has family in Folsum. An aunt, some cousins."

"What about her parents?"

Maggie paused a moment to collect her thoughts. Alice had gradually opened up to her over the months, and many of those confidences had been extremely painful. Maggie didn't want to inadvertently betray the girl.

"On a holiday binge, most likely," Maggie said finally. "At least that's what Alice said. She doesn't see them much. Ever really."

"And the aunt?"

He meant, Maggie knew, why hadn't Alice gone to live with her. "She's overburdened already. And too close to Alice's parents to allow for a comfortable day-to-day living situation."

He rolled his glass between his palms and met her eyes. "Was it worth all the trouble, Maggie? Was it worth all the energy you've expended, our fights about her?"

Maggie stiffened. "We didn't break up because of Alice."

"No, we didn't." He lowered his eyes to the glass for another moment, then lifted them back to hers. "But my question remains the same. Was it worth it?"

"Yes," she said slowly, thoughtfully. "It has been. In so many ways I'm like Alice. I could have been her, but I was lucky. I wanted, needed, to give something back. Spread the luck around, maybe." She shrugged. "I don't know exactly, but then how many people understand all their motivations?"

He was quiet a moment. "Well, whatever the reasons, you're doing something good, Maggie. I was wrong."

His words blindsided her, they were so unexpected. Tears choked her. "I was wrong, too," she whispered brokenly. "I delivered an ultimatum, when I'd had no right. I'm sorry."

"It's in the past. Forget it."

Maggie looked away, pretended interest in her food, the fire, Amanda. Seconds ticked past. *If she had waited, if she had reacted with her head instead of with blind emotion, maybe they would still be together.*

She swallowed hard. But Alice had been only the catalyst for their split, not the reason. So much had happened between them, and still somehow she didn't know what had gone wrong.

"Do you remember our first Thanksgiving together?" he asked suddenly.

Maggie met his eyes again, hoping he wouldn't notice the glassiness in her own. "How could I forget?"

Royce pushed aside his plate and leaned back on his elbows. "You insisted on the families getting to know one another...and on cooking for the whole bunch."

She smiled. "We were still in that apartment in the French Quarter."

"That *tiny* apartment in the French Quarter."

"It wasn't that small."

He looked at her in exaggerated disbelief. "For your family? That gang needs a Moose Lodge to get together comfortably."

She smiled and took a sip of wine. "True. And folding chairs aren't really your family's style."

Royce tapped the side of his nose, his lips lifting in a small smile. *"Borrowed* folding chairs. It was indeed a night for the history books."

Maggie giggled. "Remember my mother trying to talk to yours about raising children?"

Royce laughed. "My mother isn't often surprised, but your mother totally nonplussed her. She had no idea how to communicate with her. Nor could she escape." He shook his head at the image. "I can still hear her saying, 'Yes...but Nanny was in charge of potty training,' and 'Yes...but Nanny was in charge of that, too.'" He shook his head. "Then your mother tried to discuss cooking."

Maggie laughed so hard, her eyes teared. "Poor Mom. She knew your parents were in the restaurant business and thought it would be a safe subject. All she wanted was to find some common ground."

Royce laughed, too, then when Amanda stirred, he quieted his amusement. "What a mess."

"Actually, if you remember, compared to my cooking, the socializing was a big, big success."

Royce tipped his head back, fighting back another bark of laughter. "I still can't believe you didn't know you were supposed to take the neck and giblets out of the turkey. Maggie, you spent hours in the kitchen growing up. Eileen is a fabulous cook."

Maggie sniffed, feigning indignation. "I was always in charge of desserts at home. Besides, I didn't hear you offering any advice, Mr. Big-shot Restaurateur. You were there when I stuffed that bird."

He leaned toward her and wiggled his eyebrows. "I had other, more important things on my mind."

And so had she. They hadn't been able to keep their hands off one another long enough even to get the turkey into the oven on schedule.

Her tears were back, stinging her eyes, clogging her throat. "We were so much in love," she whispered. "None of it mattered."

He held her gaze. One moment became a dozen. Her mouth went dry, her palms wet. He lowered his eyes to her lips and her pulse went wild.

"No, it didn't," he said, his voice thick. "All we wanted was for the evening to end so we could make love."

Maggie swallowed against the lump in her throat. Her heart thrummed so crazily against the wall of her chest she was certain he must hear its beat. She ached. She burned. She wanted to weep for what they'd lost.

And for one dizzying moment she wondered if he would kiss her. Then he withdrew, and she thought she was going to die.

"What happened to us, Royce?" she asked, her words barely a whisper. "How did we get from that first Thanksgiving to this one?"

Royce frowned and stared into the fire. Seconds passed, the only sound between them the crackle and hiss of the fire.

"I don't know, Maggie," he said finally. "All I know is I feel like I fought a war all by myself. And I feel like I lost." He pressed a thumb and forefinger to either side of the bridge of his nose. A moment later he met her eyes once more. "Now, I'm just glad it's over."

She wrapped her arms around herself. Her chest burned with the effort of holding back tears. "Is it really over?"

"Yes, Maggie. It is."

She curled her fingers into her palms until her nails bit into the sensitive flesh. That was the difference between them—he'd put the past away, and she couldn't. Because she still loved him. Because sometimes it still hurt so damn bad she couldn't breathe.

Tears sprang to her eyes, they choked her voice. "You weren't the only one who lost, we all did. Amanda, too."

He made a sound tight with emotion. "She wasn't a part of this, of us."

"She could have been." Maggie took a deep breath, the tears brimming, spilling over. "You hurt me, Royce."

He turned to her, looked at her long and hard and evenly. When he spoke, his words were edged in steel. "God knows, that was never my intention."

"Well, you did. Badly."

He turned back to the fire. "I was always honest with you, Maggie."

"You say that as if I weren't."

"Were you? I told you in the beginning how I felt. I was up-front with you about children."

"As I was with you." She sucked in a sharp breath. "You knew how badly I wanted them."

"Yes," he said softly, "I did know."

"And you never said you didn't want them. You said you weren't sure, but you never—"

"I had my doubts," he inserted. "I told you there was a chance I'd never want them."

"Then why did you go along with me? Why did we take the first step, let alone the last?"

"You bulldozed, Maggie." He gazed at her, his eyes darkening with fury. "A more appropriate question is, Why didn't you ask me? Why didn't we discuss it? Instead, you announce that it's time to start a family. *You* took the first step, Maggie. Not *we*. I just went along with you."

Maggie curled her arms around her middle, shaking with anger and hurt. She'd been terrified that he'd say no to children. That she would be forced to choose one dream over another. That she would lose him.

In the end she'd lost him, anyway.

"No answer, Mags?" When she only shook her head, he swore and stood. "I'm getting out of here."

Tears filled her eyes, and she blinked furiously against them. The wound had been reopened; it burned. She'd been a fool to think it had healed. The dressing over it had been no more than a flimsy cover.

Sucking in a sharp breath, she stood and faced him. "Just tell me why, Royce. Why did you go through the motions, why didn't you call a halt to the whole charade?"

He laughed, the sound hard and hurting. "It's so ridiculous, really. And it should be so obvious." He met her eyes then, the expression in his bleak. "I could never refuse you anything, Maggie."

He crossed to the doorway, then stopped. Without looking back at her, he murmured, "And don't you ever be mistaken . . . you hurt me, too."

Then he was gone.

And once again Maggie was left alone and aching and staring at an empty doorway.

Chapter Five

"Hi, Maggie."

"Alice." Maggie looked up from her position on the nursery-room floor. Alice stood in the hallway, her expression troubled. Maggie smiled. "Come on in."

The girl stepped hesitantly across the threshold, then stopped and slipped off her denim jacket. Underneath she wore her A Coffee and Pastry Place sweatshirt.

Maggie grinned. "I like your shirt."

Alice didn't return the smile, but shoved her hands into the back pockets of her jeans. "I just finished my shift."

"Is everything all right?" Maggie asked. "The new girl's working out?"

"Everything's fine. Dana's okay." Alice shrugged and looked around the nursery. "What's going on?"

Maggie fought back a frown and shook the bright red rattle she held. Amanda gurgled and waved her fists. "Aerobics class."

Alice smiled then, but didn't move from her position just inside the door. "Fun."

"It is...isn't it, baby?" Maggie tapped Amanda on the nose with the rattle, and the infant gurgled again. "Join us, Alice. I'd love the company." Maggie patted the floor beside her.

Alice paused a moment, then crossed almost cautiously to where they sat. She sank down beside Maggie, taking care not to touch anything of Amanda's, not even the play quilt. "I've never seen her so awake."

"I know." Maggie laughed. "She's alert longer now. I guess that means we're starting phase two."

Alice didn't respond and Maggie continued to play with Amanda, tapping her waving fists with the toy, tickling her and making silly faces, all the while aware of Alice's silent scrutiny.

After several more moments had passed, she looked back at Alice. "How are things at school?"

The girl propped her chin on her fist. "Fine."

"How's Damon?"

"We split up."

"Oh." Maggie continued to play with Amanda, hoping her relief didn't show. "Are you okay about it?"

"I guess." Alice tugged at a piece of her spiky hair, looking at Maggie from the corner of her eyes. "He turned out to be a real creep."

Maggie frowned—with concern, but also over the fact that even after all this time together, Alice expected her to jump in with an "I told you so."

Ignoring the pinch in the vicinity of her heart, Maggie searched the younger woman's gaze. "He didn't hurt you?"

Alice looked away. "I don't hurt so easy."

After several moments of silence, Maggie touched her arm. "What's wrong, Alice?"

The girl straightened. "Why do you think something's wrong?"

"You're acting—" Maggie paused, searching for the right word. Dejected sprang to mind, as did defensive. She eliminated both. "Distracted," she said finally. "Like your mind's somewhere else and you're wishing you were, too."

"I guess that's sort of it." Alice drew her eyebrows together and looked down at her hands.

"Sort of?"

Alice lifted her chin then, meeting Maggie's gaze almost defiantly. "You like it, don't you?"

"It?"

"Being a mom."

"Yes, I do." Maggie smiled. "A lot."

"I thought so." Alice turned away, propped herself on an elbow and watched Amanda. "She is cute," she said almost grudgingly, after several moments had passed.

Maggie brushed her fingers over Amanda's soft curls. "I think she's gorgeous."

Alice reached out to touch her, too, then drew her hand back. "I wonder what..." Her voice trailed off, and she shook her head. "Never mind."

Maggie drew her eyebrows together. "Go ahead, Alice. You can tell me."

The young woman lowered her eyes, and Maggie held her breath. Seconds ticked past. Just as Maggie decided Alice was going to clam up as she had so often in the past, she murmured, "I wonder what...it would be like to be wanted like this. Like you want Amanda."

"Oh, Alice." Maggie sucked in a quick breath, emotion choking her. "You are wanted."

"Not like this." The girl shrugged, shifting her gaze again. "Forget it. It's no big deal."

It was a big deal. Maggie understood only too well how big. And Alice's attempt—her need—to pretend otherwise tore at her heartstrings. A dozen comforting words sprang to her tongue; Maggie swallowed them all. Alice would see them as empty platitudes, or worse, pity, and neither was what she needed now.

"I don't know if I'd like being a parent," Alice continued, trailing her finger experimentally along the ruffled edge of Amanda's quilt. "I mean, I probably wouldn't be any good at it."

"Why do you say that?"

"Well...you know, because of my parents."

Maggie fought the urge to pull Alice into her arms and hug her. If only she knew the right response, the one that would make Alice's pain go away.

A hug wasn't it.

Maggie swallowed past the lump in her throat. All she could give her was honesty and the wisdom gleaned from her own experiences. And pray they would be enough.

"Bad parenting," she said slowly, "isn't a genetic thing. It's behavioral. And behavior can be changed." She took a deep breath. "Your parents have an alcohol-dependency problem. That problem, that addiction, controls them and their actions."

"Yeah, I know." Alice plucked at the nap of the carpet. "But that stuff runs in families."

Maggie worked to keep her tone even, to keep the extent of her distress from showing. "The *behavior* runs in families. It's a learned behavior. You can unlearn it, Alice. You can get help, you can fight it."

Maggie could tell by the girl's stony expression that she wasn't reaching her. Alice had resigned herself to the fate of her parents. It infuriated Maggie—and it hurt. Intelligent and lovely, Alice could have a bright future ahead of her.

Or she could be caught in an ugly and destructive chain.

Maggie covered the younger woman's hand with her own. "Look at me, Alice." She paused, waiting for Alice to meet her eyes. When she did, she continued. "My parents were alcoholics, too."

She got Alice's attention with that. The girl's eyes widened, and she shook her head. "No way."

Maggie nodded. "Yes, they were. In fact, my father was killed driving drunk. He was a cabbie—when he worked."

"How come you never told me this before?"

"I don't talk about it much. I like to think that I've been able to put the past where it belongs."

"Oh." Alice frowned, her expression thoughtful. "I knew the Ryans weren't your... I mean, I knew you were adopted. But I thought—"

"That they'd adopted me as an infant."

"Yeah."

"I was five when my mother left me with them and never came back."

Alice looked down at their joined hands. "What was she like? Your real mother?"

"Eileen Ryan is my real mother."

"But... you said..."

Alice's words trailed off, and Maggie squeezed her hand, then released it. "Real mothers nurture and love and care for. They wipe tears and clean cuts and teach values. Real mothers put their own needs after those of their child. The woman who gave birth to me was the antithesis of a mother. Eileen Ryan *is* my real mother."

Alice pleated and repleated the edge of her sweatshirt. "Did you... Did that other mother hit you?"

Maggie didn't pause. "Yes."

"Did she call you names?"

"Yes. And for a long time I believed them."

Alice blinked, her eyes glassy. "And then she gave you away?"

"She deserted me, Alice. There's a difference. She hadn't the decency to 'give me away' or put me up for adoption. She didn't care enough for that."

Amanda began to fuss; Maggie scooped her up and rocked her in her arms. "It was the ultimate rejection. At least when she was abusing me, I had her attention. I understand now that it wasn't me who had a problem, that there wasn't some deficiency in me that made me unlovable." She looked down at Amanda's content and trusting face and smiled. "But feelings get twisted and tangled. All children know is that their parents are supposed to love them, and when they don't—"

"It hurts," Alice said. "Real bad."

Maggie pressed her lips to Amanda's temple, breathing in her baby scent. It was the smell of innocence and of purity; in it she found strength and a kind of peace. "Yes, it does."

Several moments passed. Alice dug her fingers into the carpet, drawing ragged, meaningless shapes in the nap, then smoothing the marks away. "What about your dad?"

"He was kinder than she. A happy drunk." Maggie smiled a little, remembering the big man who had tossed her in the air and tickled her. "Things were better when he was alive."

"So he didn't..." Alice drew in a deep breath "...you know, try to..."

She did know. And she thanked God every day she'd been spared that. Maggie gazed at the other woman, her own eyes filling with tears. Alice had been through so much in her seventeen years. And in all, she had come through it beautifully.

Maggie shook her head. "No . . . he didn't."

"I'm glad for you." Alice touched Amanda's hand lightly and with just her index finger. She smiled a little. "All that stuff about your mom, that's why it was so important for you to have a baby, wasn't it? Because you wanted to know the kind of love you didn't have."

Tears burned Maggie's throat, and she tried to swallow past them. Because of her painful experiences, Alice was wise in so many ways, had insights beyond those of other teenagers. She never failed to astound her. "Yes."

"That's cool. I mean, I can understand it. But—" Alice paused for a moment "—weren't you afraid you'd be like . . . her?"

"No." Maggie settled the sleepy Amanda onto her shoulder and gently rubbed her back. "I knew I wouldn't be. I vowed I wouldn't."

Alice cleared her throat and met Maggie's eyes. Maggie saw the naked yearning there. "How'd you get to be so strong?"

"Me? Strong?" Maggie laughed a little, pleased by the description. It was one she didn't associate with herself. "Hard work, I guess. A professional's ear when needed, lucky breaks."

"Lucky breaks," Alice repeated slowly, as if digesting it. She lifted her shoulders. "From that first day you came over and talked to me in the park, I wondered why you wanted to help. Why you took me in. It messed up your marriage and the rest of your life, too. That's it, isn't it?"

Maggie reached over and clasped her hand again. "You didn't mess up my marriage. And don't put yourself down—you're a really neat person. You deserve good things and people being nice to you."

Alice slipped her hand from hers and stood. "You always say that. And I think you really believe it." She shook her head, angry color staining her cheeks. "But anybody wouldn't have done what you did—what you're still doing. A lot of supposed good-deed doers have walked right by. My own family looked the other way. You took me in because I needed you, sure. But you needed me, too."

Maggie's breath caught as the truth—and wisdom—of Alice's words hit her. *She needed Alice.* A lump formed in her throat and she tried to swallow past it.

"Am I right?"

Even as Amanda began to whimper, Maggie nodded and lifted her eyes to Alice's. "I never thought of it that way before. But I guess you are, Alice."

A strange expression crossed the girl's face. "She's getting hungry."

"Yes." Maggie jiggled the infant to quiet her. "I'd better get her a bottle."

"I gotta go, anyway." Alice dusted off the seat of her jeans, her tone, the gesture, suddenly cocky.

Maggie frowned and followed her up. "Are you okay?"

"Yeah, fine." Alice sauntered to the door, stopping and turning back to Maggie when she reached it. "You and Mr. Royce are getting back together, aren't you?"

Maggie looked at her in shock. "Where did you get that idea?"

The young woman angled her chin up. "It's true, isn't it?"

"No." Maggie shook her head, thinking of Thanksgiving night and of the hopelessness she had felt since. She and Royce hadn't even been able to share a meal and conversation without degenerating into angry words and hurt feelings. She shook her head again. "It's not going to happen, Alice."

"Because of me."

"No. Because of Royce and me."

Alice stared at her for a moment, then turned and without another word left the room.

He'd had too damn many cups of coffee. Swearing softly, Royce let himself in the kitchen entrance of the quiet house. Nearly two in the morning and he was still wide-awake.

He shut the door behind him. Save for the illumination of the night-light, the room was dark. He reached for the overhead switch, then dropped his hand. Tonight he preferred the comfort of shadow.

Frowning, he tossed his coat over one of the ladder-back chairs. He hadn't slept well since Thanksgiving, and as much as he would like to, he couldn't blame those nights of sleeplessness on caffeine.

Only on Maggie.

Royce rubbed his hands wearily across his face. The evening they had shared had disturbed him—more than it should have and in ways he couldn't have imagined.

She had become real to him again—as he hadn't allowed her to be in a long time. For those few hours she had been his wife, the woman who had touched him as no other ever had, the one he'd married in a whirlwind of passion. But as their passion had been laid out for him to relive that night, so had their problems, intact and unplumbed.

It had been frustrating and painful... and way too close. He'd remembered the good times and the bad; he had realized—not with his head, but with his gut—what he'd had. And lost.

Annoyed with his own thoughts, Royce crossed to the refrigerator. He'd put the past, put Maggie, out of his head before, he could do it again. It was a matter of concentration, of determination and intellect. Their marriage was over, he understood his mistakes, he wouldn't lose sight of exactly why she had asked him here....

He still wanted her.

Damn it. Royce pressed the heels of his hands to his eyes in frustration. Try as he might, he could no longer rationalize away the want. And what he felt had

nothing to do with remnants of what they'd shared or
with memories. He wanted her desperately and with
every fiber of his being. At night he lay in bed sweat-
ing, unable to sleep for picturing her in the bed they
had shared, knowing only wood, Sheetrock and a
couple dozen feet separated them. His heart would
thunder uncomfortably against the wall of his chest
and his desire would burn even more uncomfortably
in his loins.

Royce breathed deeply through his nose, willing his
heart to slow, his pulse to even. This was crazy, in-
sane. He was a grown man, not an untried boy. They'd
been married, for God's sake. He knew her body almost as intimately as he knew his own.

Even so, all he had to do was think of her and he
wanted her.

He had other feelings for her, as well. Ones that
terrified him. Ones that had nothing to do with physical desire and everything to do with emotion.

He yanked on his tie, loosening it. Ridiculous! He
felt no more for her than he would for anyone in her
position. If he longed to comfort her, to kneel beside
her and rub her back, to soothe her weary muscles and
with magic fingers make her fatigue disappear, it was
only because he was, after all, a human being. He saw
the incredible amount of work caring for an infant
entailed. Maggie was getting little sleep, and during the
day she still had all her household responsibilities, plus
Alice and some baking for the coffeehouse.

He straightened, annoyed at the pinch in his chest
and at the feeling of being a fraud. She'd chosen this,

he reminded himself. She had chosen to do this on her own.

Because she had wanted it that much.

He swore and yanked open the refrigerator. Baby bottles lined the top shelf. He reached around them for his wine, then stopped. Calling himself an idiot, he took out one of the baby bottles. He stared at it a moment, weighing it in his palm, frowning.

He shook a drop of the formula onto his hand and sniffed. It smelled sweet, stronger than milk and somehow yeasty. He tasted it and made a face. How could Amanda drink this stuff?

Royce set the bottle back on the shelf, then jumped as he heard the baby cry out. He glanced at the clock. She was a consistent little tyke—it was just after two.

He reached for his wine again, then paused, looking back at the baby bottles and thinking of the shadows under Maggie's eyes. Without giving himself a chance to reconsider, he grabbed one of the bottles, warmed it in the microwave, and headed quickly upstairs.

Amanda's cries could have wakened the dead, but unbelievably they hadn't yet awakened Maggie. Royce crossed to the crib and carefully scooped up the infant. "Shh," he whispered. "It's okay, baby. I've got you."

Still she wailed. He jiggled her, imitating what he'd seen women in the restaurant do when their babies began acting up. He felt like an ox, huge and clumsy and all thumbs. And he felt like an idiot—what he knew about babies wouldn't fill a thimble.

"Shh," he repeated, jiggling her some more. "Let's let Mommy sleep tonight. She's so tired."

But Amanda wouldn't hear of it. Stiff as a board in his arms and looking mad as hell, she continued to wail.

This had been a mistake, Royce thought, suddenly panicked. A big mistake. She wanted Maggie. She knew the difference, and his arms wouldn't do.

He rocked her and hummed. She was supposed to stop crying now; he must be doing something wrong. Surely her face wasn't supposed to be so red.

Dear Lord, what was he going to tell Maggie?

Taking a deep breath, he carried her to the rocker, sat down and offered her the bottle. The minute he did, she stopped crying, grabbed onto the nipple and began to voraciously suck.

Royce stared down in shock at the infant. She made gulping sounds as she ate, tugging at the nipple in her greediness, her body quivering with tension and relief.

Shock gave way to amused wonder. He'd been doing something wrong, all right. All she'd wanted was the bottle. Poor little baby had been frantic for food.

His lips lifting, Royce trailed his fingers over her dark, downy curls. She was so tiny and trusting. So soft and sweet. A lump the size of a boulder formed in his throat. She gazed up at him as she ate, her eyes wide and unblinking, the expression in them almost one of adoration.

No one had ever looked at him like that. Not even Maggie.

He swallowed against the emotion that welled up inside him. He felt like a king. Ten feet tall and ready to conquer the world. How could she do that to him with nothing more than two big blue eyes?

He shook his head, smiling again. "Don't you know you're not supposed to look at me like that?" he whispered. "I'm just a coldhearted bastard. Ask your mommy, she'll tell you."

Amanda only blinked and Royce smiled again, cuddling her a little closer.

Minutes passed and her stomach began to fill; he saw it in the way she sucked more slowly, in the way her eyes drooped and her fists began to unclench. He smiled softly and brushed his fingers against her cheek. "My little Manda," he cooed. "How did you get to be so sweet?"

"Royce?"

With an odd sense of déjà vu, Royce lifted his head to find Maggie in the doorway watching him. In one hand she held a baby bottle, with the other she clutched her robe around her, the silky fabric clinging to and outlining her silhouette. Her hair, wild from sleep, cascaded over her shoulders and down her back.

He met her gaze then, his blood stirring. "I was up and...and I thought you could use the sleep," he murmured, his voice husky.

Maggie took a step into the room. "I heard her crying...then she stopped." She pushed the hair out of her eyes, disorientation giving way to the realization of what she'd witnessed.

He heard the breathlessness of fear in her voice. "I'm sorry if I frightened you." He cleared his throat. "I didn't think, I just..." Royce shook his head, feeling like an idiot. "That wasn't my intention," he finished stiffly.

Maggie took another step closer; tenderness welling in her chest until she thought she might burst with it. No, his intention had been to help her—despite their agreement, despite the fact that he had professed to care nothing for her or Amanda.

"Is she asleep?" she asked softly.

Royce dragged his gaze from Maggie's. "I think so...but I'm not sure."

Maggie smiled. He cradled Amanda in his arms as if he'd done it dozens of times, as if it were his right and pleasure as a father. He'd called her "his Manda."

She'd never thought him capable of this kind of tenderness.

Maggie closed the distance between them and gently tried to take the bottle from Amanda. Although she still sucked, she let the bottle be eased from her lips without resistance.

"She's beautiful, isn't she?"

Royce gazed at Maggie, his mouth dry. "Yes," he murmured, thickly. "Very beautiful."

Her pulse scrambled, and she searched his eyes. Reflected in them was something she hadn't seen in a long time, something she thought she never would again.

"What now?"

She swallowed at the double entendre. "You have to burp her."

"Like this?" He lifted Amanda to his shoulder and gently patted her back, never taking his eyes from Maggie's.

"Yes."

Seconds passed, still they gazed at one another. She broke the connection first. Trembling, she crossed to the crib and straightened the bedding, using the moments to try to collect herself, acknowledging that the moments weren't nearly enough.

She breathed deeply through her nose and told herself to be careful and smart, reminded herself of how much they had hurt each other. It was over between them; she had Amanda to think of, she . . . was aware of the exact moment he stood and moved toward her.

Then he was beside her, and together they changed Amanda's diaper, then tucked her into her bed. Maggie's head filled with him—the cadence of his breathing, the warmth emanating from his body so close to hers.

"Maggie."

On his tongue her name sounded like a prayer, and every caution she'd issued herself dissipated like so much hot air. She turned and moved into his arms.

After all this time, Maggie thought, sighing as his lips found hers. She was finally back in his arms. A shudder of pleasure ran through her and she melted against him.

His kiss was like coming home. Everything about it—the feel of his mouth as it gently explored hers, his familiar, spicy scent, the way the blood coursed roller-coaster-like through her veins at his touch.

How had she lived so long without this? Maggie wondered, curling her hands around his shoulders. How would she face tomorrow, knowing this would be denied her once more?

Tomorrow would take care of itself.

She twined her fingers in his hair and deepened the kiss.

Royce groaned. Her robe was thin, her gown thinner still. Through the fabric he felt the thundering of her heart, the tightness of her nipples. He wanted to touch, to taste all of her. He wanted her so badly he hurt.

Settling for her mouth, he caught her tongue with his, searching and possessing. He hadn't settled for less; he wasn't disappointed. She tasted as she always had—fresh and sweet and honest. She tasted like Maggie—his woman, his wife.

He moved his mouth to the curve of her cheek, the shell of her ear, his hands from her shoulders to the small of her back. And beyond. The territory was familiar, yet he delighted in the familiarity, felt relief that she hadn't changed in the time they'd been apart.

And he reveled in the sweetness of the way she molded herself to him, basked in the warmth she offered. He brought his mouth back to hers. It was as if the sun had begun to shine again, feeding his bleak world with light and heat.

Whispering her name, he lowered his hands more, cupping her, lifting her against his arousal.

Maggie moaned and tightened her fingers. She'd meant only to thank him. Not to touch, not to cling. But it had seemed so right to move into his arms, to offer him her mouth. He made her feel as she hadn't since the last time he'd held her like this—loved, protected, needed.

She stopped on the thought. Amanda needed her—Amanda loved her.

But it wasn't the same. Just as Royce's love hadn't filled the need in her for the love of a child.

Her heart wrenched and she moved her hands back to his shoulders, smoothing them over his tautened muscles, then lowering them to his chest. She flattened one hand over his heart, its beat wild under her palm.

The void hadn't been filled; the tiny place that had ached, ached still.

She needed Royce. Nothing and no one could take his place.

Tears choked her, and she pulled a fraction away from him. She searched his expression for a clue to what he felt. She understood his physical desire; she, too, burned almost out of control. She wondered what he felt with his heart.

"Royce?"

He stared at her, his breath coming quick and rough. He worked to control it even as he tightened his hands. "No words, Maggie. For now, just feel."

He didn't draw her closer, didn't move at all. The decision was hers.

Maggie squeezed her eyes shut. His voice, thick with desire, rippled over her senses, turning her knees—and her resolve—to pudding. She curled her fingers into the crisp cotton of his shirt and again offered him her mouth.

He took it with a hunger that stole her breath.

Moments became seconds became minutes. She pulled away once more, panting from the effort. "What are we doing?"

"Does it matter?"

"Yes." She flattened her hands against his chest. "More than anything."

Royce wound his fingers in her hair. She was right; it did matter. He wanted to deny her words, would love to convince her, but he couldn't lie—to either of them. He had promised himself he wouldn't become involved, had promised himself he wouldn't forget for a moment why she had wanted him with her in her home.

Yet here he was, totally involved and aching.

Making a sound of frustration and denial, he dragged her against his chest once more. Now, this moment, nothing mattered but that she be in his arms, warm and pliant and out-of-control. The future, even a second from now, he would worry over when it arrived.

He caught her lips in a bruising kiss.

Maggie's head fell back under the pressure of his mouth. This meeting was about passion, but also anger. He hated himself for wanting her. She understood because she felt the same, because she returned his kiss in kind.

It was wrong. She didn't want him in anger. Or with regrets.

She wanted what they'd had . . . and lost.

Maggie made a sound of pain, then, and he let her go. She stumbled backward, bringing a hand to her bruised mouth. "Why?" she asked brokenly, her eyes filling with tears. "Why can't we..." She let the words trail off and shook her head, fighting tears. If she said more she would reveal everything. At least now she maintained a semblance of pride.

"Oh, Mags..." Royce reached out to touch her, to soothe this time rather than excite, to comfort rather than possess.

The sound of the front door being quietly shut stopped him. He met Maggie's eyes. Hers were wide and frightened, telling him she'd heard the noise, too.

"Stay here," he ordered in a harsh whisper.

She caught his elbow. "Don't go. I'll call the police."

"Don't worry, I'm no hero." He shook off her hand. "Stay put."

As he exited the room he grabbed the big ceramic piggy bank her sister Josie had made for Amanda, and she fought back the urge to giggle. Some protection— a porker in a pink tutu.

Not about to let Royce go alone, Maggie followed, creeping several feet behind, careful to avoid the floorboards that creaked. She heard someone moving cautiously about downstairs, heard another door open and close. Her mouth went desert-dry, her palms nerve-rackingly wet.

Royce made it all the way downstairs and was out of her sight when she heard the pig crash to the floor and shatter. Her heart flew to her throat.

"Royce!"

Without pausing for thought, she raced the rest of the way down the stairs to find Royce doubled over and Alice beside him looking scared to death.

Maggie stopped, confused. "Alice?"

"Dammit, Maggie—" Royce sucked in a sharp breath "—I told you to wait upstairs."

"I didn't mean to hit him," Alice said, wringing her hands. "He startled me.... I thought he was a burglar or something."

"Ditto, here." Royce groaned and straightened slowly. "You pack quite a wallop, girl."

"But, I...don't understand. Where's the..." Frowning, Maggie looked from one to the other. "Alice, why are you down here?"

The truth hit her, then. Anger left her shaking. "It's the middle of the night, what are you doing up...and out?"

Alice jerked her chin up. "Nothing."

"Where were you?" Maggie folded her arms across her chest. "Were you with Damon?"

"I was nowhere, okay?" Alice tossed her head back defiantly. "And what were you two doing up so late? Studying for exams?"

Maggie took a step back at the sarcasm. Alice hadn't behaved like this in months. "We're not the minors in this house, Alice. And we were not the ones sneaking around.''

"Is that so?"

Alice tried to strut past, and Maggie grabbed her arm. "I won't have this kind of behavior."

"It's a free country."

Maggie fought to control her anger—and her distress. "My house, my rules."

"Then I'll go back on the street!"

"Is that what you want? Is that—''

"Maggie," Royce interrupted, laying a hand on her arm. "I'll take care of this."

Maggie swung around, furious. "Excuse me? This is my house, Alice is my responsibility. I'll take care of this . . . and everything else. Got that?"

Royce narrowed his eyes; the expression in them murderous. "Oh, I got it," he said, biting each word coldly off. "And don't worry, Maggie. I won't forget again."

Chapter Six

But he did forget. Again and again. Even as often as he called himself a fool for wanting something he recognized as no more than a fantasy, and an idiot for forgetting about the "strings attached" to Maggie's affection, he still couldn't completely reerect his guard.

Royce let himself out of the house and started across the street to the seawall. Giving in to the temptation of Maggie's mouth had been a big mistake. Now, instead of having distant memories and imagination to rationalize away, he had the real thing. Even after a week, untapped desire clung to him; he closed his eyes and he could taste and feel her, could hear her whimpers of pleasure and the hammer of his own heart.

He wanted to kiss her again. He wanted them to make love. He'd been able to think of nothing else all week.

Except for Amanda.

Royce stopped at the seawall and stared out at the turbulent lake. The day was overcast and cold, the wind biting and damp. It buffeted him, and he brought his coat collar up tighter around his neck.

He hadn't been able to ignore Amanda as he had before. All week he'd found himself wanting to hold her again, wanting to comfort her when she cried, watch her as she slept.

He couldn't forget the way he'd felt when she looked up at him with those big, trusting eyes. The scariest part was aching to feel that way again.

Royce frowned out at the lake. Sometimes he caught her looking at him and he had a sense that Amanda was saying, "I've told you how I felt about it, now the ball's in your court." Then he felt really ridiculous.

That night had changed everything. He shoved his hands into his pockets. Even Alice had begun to intrigue him. She was the last person he would have expected to feel anything for, yet he found himself at the least, curious, at the most, feeling her withdrawal and alienation as an almost palpable thing.

He'd been impressed with her progress, with the way she'd flourished under Maggie's attention. She little resembled the defiant and grimy girl Maggie had brought home nearly a year ago.

Royce pulled his hands out of his pockets and stooped to pick up a small piece of shell. He rubbed it thoughtfully between his fingers. In the light of what he'd seen since moving in, Alice's behavior of the other night didn't make sense.

"Butt out," Royce muttered to himself. "This is Maggie's family, not yours."

He drew his arm back and threw the bit of shell as far out into the rough water as he could. Without waiting to see where it hit, he turned and walked away.

Maggie watched Royce cross from the lake to the coffeehouse. She pressed her palm against the cold windowpane, not caring that it would leave a mark to clean up later. What was he thinking? she wondered. How could she hope to read his thoughts when her own were such a jumble?

She lost sight of him and turned away from the bedroom window. In the time since they'd kissed, she'd been on edge and emotional, feeling at once hopeful and hopeless. Her response to him had shaken her—even after everything that had occurred between them, he had the ability to turn her world upside-down with nothing more than a kiss.

Maggie sank onto the vanity chair. Until he'd held her in his arms again, she'd been able to pretend it was over, pretend that her head controlled her heart and body. Now all she could do was wonder how she would go on without touching him again.

Why did he have such power over her?

She gazed blankly into the mirror. It helped when she told herself she couldn't love a man who hadn't enough heart to love an innocent baby. Then, though, she would recall the softness of his expression as he'd looked down at Amanda, asleep in his arms, recall the timbre of his voice as he'd called her his little "Manda."

So she would try to reason with herself, remind herself that she wasn't the right woman for him, that they had made each other unhappy. Yet being with him felt so right. So right, that in weak moments she wanted to take the chance again, risk the rejection and prove she *was* the woman for him.

Maggie rubbed her arms, suddenly chilled. But then he would look right through her and her resolve—and heart—would break. Who was she kidding? How could she think this time around she would be any better for him than last? Neither of them had changed—she hadn't changed.

He didn't love her.

Still gazing into the vanity mirror she saw, not her own reflection, but pictures from her past: making faux pas after faux pas at Royce's social and business gatherings, the unhappiness she'd seen more and more often in Royce's eyes; his mother's face as she predicted "it" would never last. And the woman she had once called mother walking out of the Ryans' front door that final time. Without a word—not even the "mind y'rself, brat," she'd gotten so often.

Maggie wiped at the tears on her cheeks and swore. Alice had called her strong. What a laugh. She'd told Alice she was over the past. Funnier still. If either of those were true, would she be sitting here crying over ancient history?

She straightened, swiping at her cheeks again. Enough. She couldn't change any of it, not her mother's actions or the outcome of her marriage. The time had come to go on.

Jaw tight with determination, she went through the motions—she showered and dressed, applied her cosmetics. Amanda woke from her nap, and Maggie bathed and dressed her, too. Just as she started downstairs to fix a late breakfast for herself and a bottle for Manda, she heard car doors slam.

Settling Amanda on her play quilt in the parlor, she crossed to the front door and peeked out. "Mom, Dad!" she exclaimed, delighted. "What are you doing here?"

"Hi, honey," her mother called. "I hope we're not intruding."

"Not at all. In fact, you're just what I needed this gray morning. Come in."

Louise's Blazer pulled in behind her parents' car, and the twins, Jacob and Joshua, piled out almost before it rolled to a stop. A Christmas tree stuck out from the vehicle's back end. "Louise," Maggie said, "I thought you put your tree up Thanksgiving weekend."

"I did," Louise answered, grinning. "This one's for you."

Her mother crossed the shell drive. "We know you've been too busy to think about Christmas, and your father couldn't rest knowing there wasn't a tree in your living room yet." Her mother handed her a covered plate. "Cookies and fruitcake. All your favorites."

"Oh, Mom." Maggie's eyes filled with tears. Nothing could have made her feel better or luckier. She hugged the older woman. "I love you."

Eileen Ryan colored with pleasure. "I love you, too, Margaret Katherine. Now—" She rubbed her gloved hands together. "Where is that sweet baby? I can't wait to get my hands on her."

"In the parlor. Go on in." Both she and Louise started inside. "Dad," she called, "are you coming?"

"Send Royce out to help with the tree," her father boomed from the back of the Blazer.

Royce. Oh, dear. Maggie kept her smile bright through sheer will. Louise met her eyes and shrugged.

Maggie swallowed. "Can't, Dad. He—" She paused, searching for a likely place for Royce to be on a Sunday morning. At her parents' exchanged glances, she cleared her throat again. "He went to get the paper."

Louise rolled her eyes as if to say *Good one, sis. Now if he doesn't come back for a while—*

Maggie glared at her. "Come on in, Dad. I'll make coffee."

Once inside, the twins raced through the house brandishing make-believe swords, her mother drooled over Amanda, and her father and Louise argued the president's foreign policy.

She watched the clock. And prayed.

Finally she heard a key in the front door and she jumped up, smoothing a hand nervously over her navy cardigan. "That's Royce now. He's going to be so surprised to see everyone, maybe I'll just—"

"Warn him," Louise inserted dryly.

Maggie shot her sister an annoyed glance. Of course that was what she meant to do. Only she didn't intend for anyone else to know it. "Don't be silly, Louise," she said primly. "Excuse me."

She hurried to the door, getting there just as it swung open. "Royce, honey...you're back."

Royce lifted his eyebrows both at the term of endearment and at the way Maggie tucked her arm through his and led him inside.

"Guess what?" she said brightly, hearing the desperation in her own voice. "Mom and Dad stopped by." She helped him off with his coat. "They brought us a tree. Wasn't that...nice."

Before Royce could respond, Billy Ryan emerged from the kitchen. "Royce, son...how are you?" He extended his hand, and Royce fitted his own to it. "Maggie said you'd gone for the paper." He lowered his eyes. "They must have been sold out."

Royce looked at Maggie; her eyes pleaded with him to play along. He smiled. "I went for coffee. You know how fond Maggie is of her own cappuccinos."

He turned to her and handed her the small white bag. "Surprise, honey."

"Surprise," she repeated weakly, taking the bag from him and forcing a smile. "It must be the morning for them."

Royce arched his eyebrows again, then turned back to his father-in-law. "So, Billy, I hear you brought us a Christmas tree. By any chance is it that magnificent blue spruce hanging out of the Blazer?"

"You bet is is." Billy chewed on the end of his unlit cigar. "Three days before Christmas and Maggie tells us you don't have one yet." He shook his head. "Well, Mother couldn't have it, that's all. She just couldn't have it."

"Billy Ryan, you tell those kids the truth!" Eileen Ryan stepped out of the kitchen carrying Amanda, Louise and her twins following right behind her. "The man couldn't sit still knowing his new grandbaby didn't have a tree yet. I think he was afraid Santa would skip the house or something." She smiled warmly at Royce. "I hope you can forgive us our meddling."

Billy Ryan snorted. "Meddling, indeed. A grandparent's right."

Royce grinned and kissed his mother-in-law's cheek. He'd forgotten how warm Maggie's family was. And how much he liked them. "I'm glad to see you, Eileen."

The woman searched his expression for a moment, then seeming satisfied with what she saw, nodded. "We're all glad you're back, Royce."

Back? He turned to Maggie in question, but she wouldn't meet his eyes. He frowned.

"So what do you think about it so far?"

"It?" he repeated, swinging back to his mother-in-law.

"Why, about being a daddy. Your little Manda is the most precious thing." Eileen rubbed her nose against the infant's. "Maggie told us you came up with the nickname. It's adorable."

Maggie had heard him that night. How long had she been standing in the nursery doorway? Royce cleared his throat, lowering his gaze almost unwittingly to Amanda. She looked back up at him and gurgled. He swore silently. This situation had gotten way too complicated. "Yes, she's . . . adorable."

"I don't mean to hog her." Eileen held her out. "I guess I can share with Daddy."

Royce stiffened. "I hold her all the time, Eileen. Grandma needs a turn, too. Could you excuse us for a moment? I need to talk to Maggie in private." He turned toward her and motioned to the kitchen. "Darling?"

Louise stepped in with a story of the twins' pranks of the night before. Heart hammering and palms damp, Maggie followed him. "I can explain," she whispered as the kitchen door swung shut behind them.

"Really?" he snapped, facing her.

"Yes . . . I—"

"You lied. You told them we were back together."

"Well . . . yes." She clasped her hands together. "But I had a good reason." He only stared at her, and she colored. "Royce, they wouldn't have understood. It would have hurt them."

"And how are they going to feel when the adoption's final and the marriage is over . . . again?"

"I'll worry about that then. I'll—"

"No, Maggie, you'll tell them the truth. Now."

"I can't." She shook her head. "Not yet."

"Then I will."

He started for the door, but she caught his arm a moment before he reached it. "Royce... please. I'm begging you."

He paused, his resolve, as always when it came to Maggie, beginning to crumble. He steeled himself against the weakness. "Dammit, Maggie. I don't like this. I don't like lying to your family."

She released a shaky breath. "I don't, either."

"But to do so was *your* choice. You thought it would be easier. For *you*, Maggie." He shook off her hand and crossed to the kitchen window. The gray sky had darkened to slate, the wind bent the branches of the ancient oaks.

He swung back around, facing her again. "Once more, you didn't consider how I might feel. I like your family. I don't feel right about lying to them. And I don't appreciate knowing that when this is all said and done, I'll be the bad guy. It isn't fair."

Maggie looked away. He was right; she hadn't considered his feelings. As always she'd forged ahead, relying on her gut and heart. "I thought your paths wouldn't cross," she whispered. "I thought..." She shook her head. "I didn't think, Royce. I'm sorry."

In the other room, Amanda began to cry. "She wants a bottle." Maggie lifted a hand and saw that it trembled. "I'd better—"

"I'll get the bottle." He motioned to the door. "Go ahead, go take care of her."

Maggie crossed to the door, then stopped. "Royce?"

He looked at her and muttered an oath at the pleading in her eyes. "Okay, I'll play along. For now."

The day passed in a flurry of noise, activity and laughter. Royce helped Billy get the tree up, then rummaged in the attic for the ornaments. Maggie made eggnog and Eileen and Louise whipped up a huge pot of spaghetti. Somehow the word got out that it was family day at the Adlers' and a dozen other Ryans showed up for the fun.

By evening Royce found himself sleepy but surprisingly contented. And relaxed for the first time in what seemed like forever.

Maggie was relaxed, too. He leaned back in the big armchair and watched her and her sisters hang ornaments on the tree. They stepped back to judge the placement of each, arguing amiably over the others' choices and opinions. Every once in a while one of the brothers would pipe in with their opinion and the three sisters would simultaneously turn up their noses at the suggestion.

What a family this was. Loud and warm and sometimes obnoxious. But always loving. He thought of his and Honoria's civility toward one another, of their cool acceptance of siblinghood. Was it that they didn't love each other or that they didn't know how?

Royce shook off the question and moved his gaze around the room before settling it back on Maggie.

With her flawless skin and midnight hair, she was the exotic in this sea of freckled redheads. That she wasn't "flesh of their flesh" was obvious; he'd often wondered if growing up she had felt a part of them, or different and disconnected. As Alice did.

He frowned at the thought, and glanced at Alice from the corners of his eyes. Like him, she sat apart from the group, her expression one of sulky boredom. That expression, he suspected, hid as much as it protected. He started to stand and go to her, when he heard the musical sound of Maggie's laughter.

She tipped her head back; her throat formed a sensual arc against her dark curtain of hair. His gut tightened. He wanted to trail the tips of his fingers along that arc, to feel her quiver under his touch, wanted to bury his fingers in her hair, his body in hers.

Maggie turned and looked at him then, holding up a lumpy, little angel ornament they'd bought at a school fair and had laughed over every Christmas since. Their eyes met; her smile faded. As in every sappy romantic movie he'd ever seen, the world around him seemed to blur and fade until there was only Royce and Maggie and the current of energy crackling between them.

Maggie's sister nudged her and the connection shattered. It had lasted a second only; he felt, ridiculously, as if it had changed his world forever.

"I think I'll join the girls," Eileen murmured, still holding the sleeping Amanda. "Can you take her?"

Royce dragged his gaze from Maggie to his mother-in-law. He blinked. "Pardon me?"

She smiled and stood. "Amanda. Can you watch her?"

He cleared his throat. "Of course," he murmured. "I'd...love to."

She carefully placed the sleeping Amanda in his arms. The infant stirred and whimpered her protest; he automatically murmured soft words and stroked her head.

The rest of the evening melted away. He didn't meet Maggie's eyes again; although he was unsure whether by his design or hers.

One by one, Maggie's family left. Alice slipped away without a word; Amanda slept soundly in the nursery. Finally Maggie and Royce were alone beneath the colorful twinkling lights of the tree.

Maggie laced her fingers together; they trembled, but so did every other part of her body. She tried to quell the shudders; she told herself she wasn't a giddy sixteen-year-old.

She wanted him to kiss her so badly she hurt.

"Well..." She had no idea what to say to him. What she wanted to say was out of the question. She peeked at him and her cheeks heated at the intensity of his gaze. "The tree turned out great," she murmured quickly, breathlessly. "It was nice of Mom and Dad to bring it."

"Very," he said softly. "But then, your parents are nice people."

She looked at him again, then away. Her heart beat so heavily she wondered if he could hear it. "I had a lot of fun tonight, and I want to...you know...thank you. I was out of line before and—''

''Maggie?''

She turned to him, and he lowered his eyes to her mouth. ''Yes?'' she whispered.

''I don't want to make small talk.'' He took a step toward her.

She swallowed, her throat parched. ''No?''

''No.'' He shook his head and took another step.

''I suppose I should...Amanda will be waking up soon and...'' Her voice caught as he reached out and trailed his fingers along the curve of her throat.

''And?'' he murmured.

''I should go.''

''Then go.''

She didn't move a muscle.

He caught a piece of her hair and rubbed it between his fingers. ''I've wanted to do this all night.'' He brought the hair to his mouth and brushed it against his lips. ''So soft,'' he whispered, meeting her eyes. ''So fragrant.''

She bit back a moan, but stood stock-still, afraid if she moved he would stop. He brought his hand to the side of her face, brushing his thumbs over her cheekbones. Warm, slightly rough, they grazed her flesh. She felt the touch like a brand.

Whimpering, she tipped her face into the caress. She wanted him so badly she trembled with the need. Now, at this moment, she cared nothing about tomorrow or consequences—only that she relieve the ache inside her.

He plunged his hands into her hair, stroking her scalp, dragging his fingers through the long strands. Her head fell back and he pressed his lips to her throat.

A sound of surprise and pain wrenched them apart. It came from neither of them. Royce lifted his head; a second later Maggie heard his muttered oath. She wheeled around in time to see Alice race up the stairs.

"Oh, no." Maggie plummeted back to reality. She looked at Royce; she saw that he, too, had come back to earth. His expression aloof, almost angry, he dropped his hands and stepped away from her.

"Don't, Royce," she whispered, reaching up and touching his cheek, needing the comfort of connecting with him once more.

"What?" he returned, his tone harsh. "Get involved with your family?"

She pulled her hand back, hurt. "That wasn't fair."

"On the contrary, it was quite fair."

"Don't shut me out."

"How could I, Maggie?" he asked stiffly. "Those doors were closed and locked a long time ago. By both of us."

She drew in a deep breath, meeting his gaze defiantly. "Dammit, Royce. You started this."

"I know." He began to turn away from her. "I shouldn't have."

She caught his arm. "What's going on? Why are you doing this?"

He lifted his eyebrows coolly. "I don't know what you mean."

"Yes, you do." She tightened her fingers on his arm. "What's going on with us? If those doors are closed, what are we doing here?"

He stared at her for what seemed like minutes but could only have been seconds. Finally, softly, he said, "We're playing house, Maggie. We got caught up in the game." Without another word, he turned and left the room.

Maggie watched him go, her chest tight with unshed tears. "How can you call this a game?" she whispered brokenly to the now-empty doorway. "How can you call it a game, when I call it love?"

Helplessly she turned back to the twinkling lights of the tree, their festive colors blurring through her tears.

Chapter Seven

The next morning Royce awakened to the sound of Amanda crying. He glanced at the clock, then pulled himself out of bed even though it was barely six. There was no way he was going to be able to go back to sleep. Every time he closed his eyes he saw Maggie as she'd been in his arms, then as she'd looked the moment before he'd turned and walked away.

He rubbed his hands over his face. He hadn't slept well; he'd tossed and turned for hours after he'd come up the night before. Maggie's question, and his own response to it, had kept rolling around in his head, plaguing him.

He was, indeed, getting caught up in the game— with Maggie, her baby, Alice. It had to stop.

Royce scowled. Coffee. He needed coffee—hot, black and bracing. He pulled on jeans and a sweater, then went in search of a cup.

Maggie was in the kitchen, juggling both Manda and the phone. She wore a pair of white sweats he remembered from years ago, the white now less than bright, the fabric worn and clinging. The way it clung—and the curves it clung to—was damn distracting, and he lifted his eyes to her face. She had fastened her hair back with a big silver clip. She looked tense and tired.

Even as he wondered what was going on, he told himself to butt out. Fixing his gaze on the coffeepot, he crossed to it and poured himself a cup.

"...understand. Don't worry about it, Louise." She paused. "You talked to Josie, too? And Pete?" She paused to listen again. "It'll be fine... Okay... Sure.... I hope they feel better. You, too. Bye."

Maggie replaced the receiver and blew out a long, frustrated breath. "Damn."

Don't ask. Whatever was going on, it wasn't his problem. He opened the paper and pulled out the financial section. But instead of reading it, he slid a glance at Maggie from the corners of his eyes. She hadn't moved in the moments since she'd hung up the phone, nor had her worried expression become any less troubled.

Not his problem.

She sighed. Once, then twice.

Royce swore silently and called himself a fool. "What's wrong?"

Maggie looked at him coolly. "Nothing that I can't handle." She tilted up her chin. "Thanks, anyway."

He supposed he deserved her haughty attitude after last night, but it infuriated him, anyway. He snapped the paper back open. "Have it your way."

"Thank you, I will."

"Fine."

Still she didn't move. She sighed again. He lifted his head and glared at her. "Dammit, Maggie. Just tell me what's wrong."

She glared right back. "I have enough to worry about this morning. The last thing I need to deal with is your foul mood."

"Well, excuse me for trying to help." Furious, he made a great show of going back to the paper.

Amanda began to cry and Maggie made a sound of distress. "What's wrong with you, Manda?" she asked softly, rubbing the infant's back. "Didn't you get enough sleep? Or did you wake up on the wrong side of the crib?"

Royce frowned and glanced around the newspaper. Amanda looked uncomfortable and unhappy, and her whimpers tore at his heartstrings. "Is something wrong with the baby?"

"I don't know," Maggie murmured. "She was up most of the night just being fussy, and when she did sleep, it was fitfully. Her mood's no better today."

No wonder Maggie looked so tired this morning. Royce moved his gaze from Maggie back to Amanda. She had settled down again and looked as if she were asleep. "Maybe she had too much excitement yesterday."

"That's what I'm guessing. It was a big day." Maggie drew her eyebrows together. "But now I don't know what to do. I have—" She shook her head and looked away. "Never mind. I can take care of it myself."

Royce sighed and put the paper aside. He was a first-class idiot...but he couldn't not ask. "Take care of what, Maggie?"

She jutted her chin out. "I wouldn't want you to get too caught up in 'the game.'"

The woman was infuriating. He'd forgotten how stubborn she could get when mad...or hurt. And she was both this morning. Even though he knew it was a mistake, he shoved aside his vow to get uninvolved.

"Amanda seems content now," he said softly. "Take her upstairs, rock her for a while, then put her to bed. She'll be fine after she gets some more rest."

"That's what I *should* do." She caught her bottom lip between her teeth. "But Jonathan and Joshua are sick and Louise can't find anyone to stay with them. Nor can she find anyone to take her stint at the coffeehouse. Everybody's tied up until afternoon."

"What about Alice?"

"She's already scheduled, and even slow mornings are too much for one person." Maggie shifted Amanda to a more comfortable position on her shoulder and frowned. "Manda and I are going to have to go in. I just hope she lets me get cleaned up—

every time I've put her down this morning she's begun to cry."

Not your problem, man. Leave it alone.

"Give her to me, Maggie. I'll watch her while you dress." The offer spilled out before he could stop it.

Maggie looked at him, obviously torn, then tilted her chin up. "Thank you," she said stiffly. "But I can't impose."

Stubborn, he thought again. Royce narrowed his eyes. "Look, Maggie, if it had been an imposition I wouldn't have offered. You need to get dressed and you can't do it with a baby perched on your shoulder."

"She might start to cry again."

"We'll never know if we don't give it a try." Royce held his arms out. "Come on, Maggie."

Hesitantly, she placed Amanda in his arms. As soon as she did, the infant began to howl. "This isn't going to work," Maggie said, her voice tight with frustration and exhaustion. "Give her back."

"Give it a minute." Ignoring Maggie's outstretched arms, he lifted Amanda to his shoulder and imitated what he'd seen Maggie do a moment ago. Still she cried, but more softly.

"What's going on?" Alice walked into the kitchen, rubbing her eyes and yawning. She saw Royce and stiffened. "Oh, it's you."

Royce arched his eyebrows. "Good morning to you, too."

Alice turned her back on him. "What's wrong with Manda?"

"She's a little crabby today," Maggie answered defensively, snatching the infant away from Royce and trying to quiet her. "To make matters worse, Louise can't come in this morning and Dana won't. No one else panned out, so it's up to me and Amanda. But as you can see, Amanda's acting strangely and I'm afraid—"

"I'll go," Royce said. "Sassy's is closed today and my paperwork can wait."

Alice made a sound of disgust. "I can handle it myself. I'll be better off without *him*, anyway—I'd just spend all my time showing him what to do."

"It's going to be busy, Alice," Maggie said. "With the kids out of school for the holidays and so many people out shopping..." Maggie let her words trail off.

"I can handle it, Maggie." Alice glared at Royce. "Really, I can."

"Amanda and I will go."

That Alice was so adamant he not go, made him all the more determined to. Curiosity, Royce told himself. Nothing more.

"Don't be ridiculous, Maggie," he said, shaking his head. "How much help do you think you're going to be with a crying child on your hip?"

"Amanda *would* be better off at home," Maggie murmured.

"Yes, she would be," he repeated for emphasis. "There's no reason you should drag her out today, when I'm here and willing."

Maggie sighed. "If you're sure..."

"I am."

Alice opened her mouth to protest again, then snapped it shut as Amanda began to cry. After shooting him a glance that said, You can come, but if you think I'm going to be nice to you, you've got another think coming, she stalked out of the kitchen.

Alice *wasn't* nice. As a matter of fact, she didn't say more than a handful of words to him in the first three hours they worked together. And the words she did disdainfully mutter had only to do with A Coffee and Pastry Place's procedures.

Royce didn't mind Alice's surliness. The coffee-house was as busy as Maggie predicted—at times. At others it was deadly slow. During the slow spells he used the time to study the teenager. What he saw surprised him. She was great with the customers. Gone were all traces of sarcasm and sulkiness; she was friendly, efficient and quick to supply an interesting fact about their product.

During one of those times, Royce stood with his back to her listening to her as he foamed milk for a cappuccino.

"...people think espresso has more caffeine than a dark-roast, a dark-roast more than a medium-roast, but the opposite is true. The longer the bean roasts, the more caffeine burns off."

Royce scooped the milk onto the top of the coffee, dusted it with cocoa, then handed it to the customer. After he'd rung it up, he turned to Alice. "I didn't know that."

"What?" She didn't look at him.

"About the caffeine amount in the various roasts."

"Listening to other people's conversations is tacky."

Royce ignored that. "I've heard you share a lot of other coffee facts this morning. Where do you pick up all this?"

"I *can* read." She turned toward him then, her shoulders stiff and her jaw tight with dislike. "Maybe you should try it."

"Okay, Alice." He placed his fists on his hips and faced her. "What's your beef?"

"I don't know what you're talking about."

"Like hell. You haven't said a dozen words to me all morning, and when you do speak it's obvious that you'd like me dead. Why do you dislike me so?"

"What's to like?"

He smiled a little, amused rather than offended. "You've got a point there."

She looked surprised at his reaction, then she narrowed her eyes. "I know what's going on between you and Maggie. I'm not a stupid child."

"No? Then why are you acting like one? Why the stunt the other night?"

"Why the third degree?" she shot back. "You're not my guardian. Maggie is." She lifted her chin cockily. "*You're* just temporary."

She was right. He wasn't her guardian, he *was* only temporary. He'd told himself the same a dozen times. But for whatever reason, she interested him, and he couldn't let it go.

Something about Alice reminded him of himself.

Royce stopped on the thought, then pushed it away. "You said you knew what was going on between me and Maggie? Maybe you should fill me in, because I'm damn confused."

She stared at him a moment, angry spots of color staining her cheeks. "You're jacking her around," she said, finally. "And I don't like it. Leave her alone."

She said the last almost ferociously, and Royce knew what he'd already suspected: Maggie had a fierce champion in Alice.

He arched an eyebrow. "How do you know I'm not the one who's being jacked around?"

"Because Maggie wouldn't do that." Alice folded her arms across her chest. "Besides, you rich types have so much, you can't stand for there to be something you can't have."

Her comment struck a nerve; anger was on him so suddenly he shook with it. "You think I have everything, Alice?"

"Don't you?" she shot back. "Fancy suits and foreign cars and houses on the lake. You wouldn't know need if it slapped you in the face."

Furious, Royce met her gaze. "What makes you think it hasn't already? What makes you think you're the only one with a sad story to tell?"

"Oh, sure," Alice sneered. "Poor little rich dude. My heart bleeds."

"Did it ever occur to you," he said softly, carefully, "that maybe Maggie has more than I do? That she always has?"

Alice tried to swing away from him and he caught her arm. "What about love, Alice?"

"Give me a break!" She shook off his hand, but didn't try to move away. "That old cliché about money not being able to buy love ... it was probably started by a rich dude just like you."

He met the girl's eyes again, his own, he knew, were cold with fury. "I look at her family and I wonder what it would have been like to be one of them. To know I could depend on any of them and that they wouldn't let me down. To know I was supported and loved ... no matter what I did."

"You have a family."

Royce laughed, the sound hard. "Yes, I have a family. So do you." He dropped his hand. "And I'd bet all I own that neither one of us puts ours in the same class as Maggie's."

"You don't know anything!" Alice balled her hands into fists. "Not about me...not about how I lived. Did you wear clothes that weren't much better than rags because your parents used every penny to buy booze? Or did you spend every birthday alone, every holiday hiding behind the couch or in a closet, hoping that this year they would pass out early and not come looking for you? Did you have to endure the snickers of the other kids or the hell of not having any friends?"

She met his eyes, then. Although hers were glassy, she held her head high. "Did you?"

Royce's heart wrenched, but he kept his feelings from showing. Alice didn't need sympathy or pity from him. She could spend the rest of her life wallow-

ing in both, just as her parents had wallowed in booze
and his had in greed and selfishness.

"You're right, I don't know. I couldn't." He took
a step toward her. "But I do know there are all kinds
of abuse, all kinds of neglect."

"I've got tables to bus."

"My parents," he continued softly, "were so busy
buying things—including people and affection—they
forgot about being human. And God knows they
never knew anything about being parents. Like how to
give, to feel, to care. Power mattered, as did prestige
and appearances."

Alice paused and turned almost grudgingly back to
him.

"Yeah, I had everything—everything material. And
yeah, your childhood was a hell of a lot tougher than
mine. But I wanted love. I wanted admiration from my
parents or a show of pride in my accomplishments.
And like you, I didn't get those things. I never will."

Royce stopped. He hadn't meant to deliver an ora-
tion on his childhood, hadn't known even that those
words were there. He'd wanted only to get to the root
of Alice's recent behavior. This had nothing to do with
him, had nothing to do with . . .

He let the thought die and shifted his gaze back to
Alice's. She looked as surprised as he felt. And as affected. They stared at each other a moment, then she
jutted her chin out. He saw that it trembled.

"If you're trying to get me to like you," she said,
her voice huskier than before, "you can forget it."

She said the words as if she would stake her life on them. But the tremble and something in her eyes suggested that she had already begun. Royce wasn't sure why that made him feel so good; it shouldn't have.

But it did. Damn good.

More uncomfortable with that truth than any of the ones he'd spoken moments before, he cleared his throat. "You don't have to like me, Alice," he said quietly. "Only yourself."

Maggie awakened with a start. Amanda, she acknowledged. Again. She jumped out of bed and threw on her robe, stumbling in the dark.

She couldn't be hungry, Maggie thought, racing into the nursery. She'd had a bottle an hour ago and hadn't even taken much of that.

Her heart began to thrum crazily against the wall of her chest. Amanda's cries sounded different, less angry and more choked.

Something was wrong.

"Sweetheart," she murmured, reaching the crib, "it's Mommy. What's wrong, baby?" She scooped her out of her bed and gasped. Amanda's skin was hot. She was burning up with fever.

Oh, God...Oh, God...Maggie lifted Amanda to her shoulder and began to walk the room, rubbing her back and trying to quiet her, trying to think.

"Quiet, sweetie," she whispered, holding her panic in check. "Shh...It's okay. Mommy will—"

Maggie stopped at that. She had no idea what to do. Dear lord, what if she'd already done something wrong? What if—

Stay calm, she told herself, her mind going completely blank except for blind terror. She tried to push the fear away, she told herself that Manda needed her calm and rational, but the "what if" kept worming its way back into her head, paralyzing her.

If only she could think. If only she could be logical and calm and...

Royce. She needed Royce. He would know what to do.

Turning, she raced out of the nursery and down the hall, Amanda's cries sounding weak and hurting. Please let him be there, she prayed. Please.

He *was* there. She almost sobbed with relief when she saw his sprawled form under the covers. She ran across the room. "Royce...wake up." She reached out to shake him and saw how badly her hand trembled. Sucking in a sharp breath, she put her hand on his arm. "Royce...wake up."

The minute she touched him, he sprang awake.

"Maggie?" He stared at her as if he thought he was dreaming. He shifted his gaze from hers to the crying Amanda. "Maggie?" he said again.

"Royce...you have to help.... I don't know..." Tears choked her words.

He jumped out of bed, instantly awake. "My God, what's wrong?"

"It's Manda," Maggie sobbed. "She's burning up. I've tried to quiet her, but she won't and I...don't know what to do."

Royce touched Amanda's cheek, then snatched back his hand, alarmed. He worked to control his own panic. "Have you taken her temperature?"

"No." Maggie shook her head. "I wanted to try to quiet her first and I—"

"Have you called the pediatrician?"

"It's the middle of the night...and I didn't know if I—"

"That's what she gets paid for," Royce said grimly, stepping around her for his robe. He slipped into it, then turned back to her. "What's her number?"

"It's in my book...in the bedroom." She followed him, her heart beginning to slow its frenetic beat. She drew in a deep, shuddering breath, the oxygen calming her. "The doctor will want her temperature. The thermometer's in our bathroom."

Royce didn't comment on her word choice, although he felt it like a punch to his gut.

They took Manda's temperature. Unbelieving, Royce looked at the thermometer twice, then met Maggie's eyes. "One hundred and five," he said quietly.

"There must be some mistake," Maggie whispered, holding Amanda tighter. "That's so hot... so—"

"There's no mistake, Maggie. Get the pediatrician's number. Now."

Royce called. While he described Amanda's condition and behavior of earlier that day to the doctor, he watched Maggie walk and rock Manda. The infant's cries had become fitful mewls, and he found the tiny, helpless sounds more terrifying than her earlier howls. Maggie felt the same—he saw it in her eyes when she looked at him.

He jerked his attention back to what the doctor was saying. "I understand. Thank you."

Royce hung up and turned back to Maggie, her face a study in fear. He knew his looked just as grim. "From what I told her, she suspects an ear infection. They're common in infants, pop up suddenly and are accompanied by high temperatures."

"Thank, God." Maggie squeezed her eyes shut. "Thank—"

"But," Royce inserted quickly, not wanting Maggie to become falsely reassured, "a high fever is also indicative of many other less common and more serious illnesses. We've got to get her temperature down. Do you have any acetaminophen? Not aspirin, Maggie."

"I think so..." She nodded her head. "Yes, I do. I'm sure."

"Good. We give her a dose, wait an hour, then take her temperature again. If that doesn't bring it down to about normal, we have to give her a tepid bath. If that doesn't work..."

He paused and Maggie's heart stopped. "Yes?"

''We go to the emergency room. Her temperature is high, Maggie. Bordering on dangerous. It's critical that it not go up.''

They gave her the acetaminophen, then took turns walking her. During the tense hour neither of them spoke; the only sounds in the room were their murmurings to Amanda and the old floorboards creaking as they moved back and forth across them.

Just about the time Maggie thought she would scream from the tension of not knowing, Royce announced that the hour was up. Maggie held her breath as he took Amanda's temperature, even though she knew it hadn't lowered nearly enough.

''One hundred and four point five.''

Maggie tried to hold back her cry of fear and frustration; it escaped anyway. ''This is all my fault,'' she said brokenly. ''If I'd recognized the signs, if I'd been less concerned with the coffeehouse and more concerned with Amanda's odd behavior, I would have taken her to the doctor. I *should* have taken her. If only I'd—''

''Stop it, Maggie,'' Royce said sharply. ''This is no one's fault. How could you know? You've never been a mother before—''

''But I grew up in a house full of children. I was a sister and helped care for the little ones.''

''It's not the same and you know it. And you've never cared for an infant before.'' When she opened her mouth as if to protest again, he added, ''It doesn't help Manda for you to whip yourself. She needs our calm action now, not self-recriminations and self-pity.''

Heat stung her cheeks even though she knew he was right. She met his eyes, her own filling with tears.

''It'll be all right, Maggie. It will.'' He caught her elbow. ''Come,'' he said softly, ''I'll draw the bath.''

Maggie held Amanda while he filled the tub. His hands shook as he adjusted the faucets, as he tested the water. That done, he turned. And froze. Maggie had slipped out of her robe and gown, and stood gloriously nude before him. He moved his gaze over her before he could tell himself not to, before he could drag it away. Her flesh seemed as rosy as Manda's in the soft light of the bathroom and, swallowing hard, he brought his eyes back to hers. ''The water's ready.''

She nodded, and wordlessly stepped into the tub. Amanda fussed as the cool water touched her fevered skin, but Maggie made no sound at all.

They didn't look at one another, they didn't speak. Royce sponged them with the water. Cool for Maggie, gooseflesh ran up her arms and over her chest as the water sluiced over her and her nipples hardened into tight little buds.

But the water quieted Amanda, and her skin began to lose its fevered flush. Minutes later she was asleep in Maggie's arms.

Royce took her temperature. ''Almost normal.''

Maggie let out a shuddering breath. ''Thank God.''

''I'll dry her while you...get...dressed.'' The words caught in his throat; keeping his gaze averted was almost physically painful. Maggie was his wife; there had been a time when he would have looked at her for as long as he liked, and she would have returned his gaze just as boldly, both of them wanting.

Had it been so long ago? It seemed like yesterday.

He handed Maggie a towel for herself and took Amanda, then turned his back to her.

Several moments later she cleared her throat. "You can turn around now."

He did, but instead of seeing her bundled up in her white chenille robe, he saw her as she'd been the moment before she stepped into the tub. The image, the memory, made him ache. As if she could read his thoughts, color slid up her cheeks until she glowed with it.

He dragged his gaze back to Amanda, still wrapped in the fluffy towel. "We better get her dressed."

"Yes."

They took the infant back to the nursery, quickly getting her into her sleeper and under the covers.

Maggie curled her fingers around the top of the crib rail, squeezing so tightly her fingers went numb. She stared down at her sleeping daughter, tears filling her eyes. "What if I'd lost her?" she whispered, the tears spilling over. "What if—"

"Shh." Royce put his hands on her shoulders and gently massaged her tense muscles. "You didn't, you won't."

Maggie leaned back against him, taking comfort in his strength, his reliability. His heart beat steadily behind her shoulder blade, and she closed her eyes. "I don't know what I would have done without you. All I could think was what if... what if..." She shuddered. "It was so awful. I don't ever want to go through this again."

He rubbed his cheek against her hair, breathing in the scent of her perfume mixed with that of the bath. "I know, baby. I know."

Maggie drew in a tired breath. "I love her so much. I don't know if I could go on without her."

His heart twisted. Yet she'd gone on without him so easily. "You don't have to worry about that. It's not going to happen.... Nothing's going to happen."

She tipped her head back and met his eyes. "Maybe I'm not cut out to be a mother. The way I panicked—" The tears were back, filling her eyes, choking her.

"You were exhausted, you still are." He smoothed the dampened tendrils of hair away from her face. "You need some sleep, Maggie."

"No." She turned back to her daughter and lightly touched her downy cheek. Her flesh was still cool to the touch. Maggie shook her head. "I can't leave her."

"You're dead on your feet." He moved his fingers slowly and rhythmically over her shoulders. "It'll be dawn soon and she's sleeping soundly. Come."

Maggie resisted. "What if she needs me?"

"She'll let you know." He smiled a little. "Maggie, this child has a very healthy set of lungs." When she still hesitated, he dropped his hands to hers and loosened them from the crib rail. "Manda needs you alert and calm. She needs a mommy who's had enough sleep to function."

Always so rational, Maggie thought foggily, turning and allowing him to lead her from the nursery. So in control. Those didn't seem such bad things now, didn't seem so infuriating.

Royce helped her out of her robe and into bed, then tucked the blankets around her. Unable to stop himself, he leaned down and brushed his lips across hers. They were warm and slightly parted; it took all his self-control to break the contact. "Get some sleep," he murmured. "Everything's okay now."

"Is it?" she whispered, trembling still. She looked up at him, searching his expression. She felt so safe with him. Protected and cherished. She didn't want him to go.

But it was what she read in his eyes that made her heart flutter. "Royce?" she whispered.

"Yes?"

"Don't leave me." She circled his neck with her arms. "Stay."

Her words affected him like a dizzying punch to his solar plexis. Royce drew in a swift, agonized breath. "I'm not going any place, Maggie. I'll be right down the hall if you need me."

"No." She searched his gaze. "Stay with me here. In this bed, our bed. I need you to hold me."

Royce swallowed, his mouth, his throat, suddenly parched. As he was parched for her touch, starved for her warmth. He took in her still-frightened gaze, the exhaustion around her eyes and mouth. She needed him for comfort, for security. And at this moment he needed her for so much more.

"No, Maggie." He shook his head and drew away from her. "Tonight I can't give you what you need."

Chapter Eight

Maggie tightened her arms around his neck, clinging to him. "I haven't asked anything of you but that you stay," she whispered. "How can you not be able to give me that?"

And how could he tell her that was exactly why he couldn't stay? He caught her hands, taking her arms from around him. "Maggie, you were badly frightened. You're exhausted—"

"Please," she begged. "Please stay."

He searched her expression. "If I do, I can't promise you—"

"No promises," she said quickly. "Nothing but your warmth, your arms."

Unable to help himself, he brushed his mouth over hers once more, the lightness of the touch an agony only outdone by the ending of it. "All right, Maggie," he murmured, his voice thick. "I'll stay."

He shrugged out of his robe and slipped into the bed beside her. He wrapped his arms around her and cradled her against his chest.

Nothing had felt so right in a long time.

Moments became minutes as he held her, her face nestled in the crook of his chin, her hands resting on his chest. He wondered if she could feel the wild pump of his heart there in his breast; wondered, too, if she knew how he felt, what he wanted, if she would run or welcome.

He held himself perfectly still, fearing that once he moved against her he would no longer be able to control his need. Warmth emanated from her. And sweetness. They filtered over and surrounded him like magic pixie dust. She made him believe he could fly. She always had.

The truth of that shook him to his core.

Maggie breathed deeply, his scent filling her head, her senses. Tenderness overwhelmed her. This man who said he cared nothing for Amanda had been terrified tonight. He had tried to hide it, he'd stayed calm and rational—but she'd seen the fear, seen the "what ifs" in his eyes, heard them in his voice.

She smiled a little and moved her mouth across his shoulder. He'd lost his heart to Manda. She didn't know when it had happened, only that it had.

He was the man she'd always thought him to be.

If only she could be the woman he needed. If only she could make him love her again.

Her muscles loosened, liquefied. Fear and exhaustion eased, giving way to awareness. She moved against him, giving and receiving comfort, telling him, without words, of her feelings. Her needs.

Maggie lowered her mouth, trailed it across the hard pebble of his nipple. It stiffened more under her lips; she felt him tremble, heard his sharply indrawn breath.

"Maggie..."

"Mmm?" She brushed against him once more, this time her thigh against his manhood. He was hard and, she knew, aching. He radiated heat like a furnace.

He wanted her as much as she wanted him.

In this one way, at least.

She pushed that thought aside, choosing instead to revel in the fact that he still desired her, that she still had the ability to arouse him to such a pitch so quickly.

She put her hand where her leg had just been.

"My God, Maggie," he rasped. "Do you know what you're doing?"

"Making love with my husband," she answered, moving her fingers, stroking.

He groaned and slid his hands down her back, over the silky fabric of her gown, stopping at the swells of her bottom. He cupped her and fitted her to him, trapping her pelvis against his, her hand against his arousal.

Joy shuddered through her. He wouldn't refuse her. He couldn't.

Royce caught her mouth in a searing kiss. Her lips, already warm, became warmer. Softly parted, she parted them more. She offered her tongue boldly and without hesitation.

He took what she offered, even as he told himself it was a mistake. With every fiber of his rational self, he knew he would regret in the morning, as would she. Now, this moment, he was crossing the line between being simply caught up in the game and being a full-fledged player.

But the part of him that could still intellectualize was small, indeed. Everything else burned, and had for weeks. He wanted with a ferocity that stunned him, needed to bury himself in her warmth with a single-mindedness that bordered on obsession.

Stopping was an impossibility. The regrets would wait until tomorrow.

Bringing his hands to her hair, he tangled his fingers in the midnight strands, deepened the kiss and lost himself in her.

Maggie held onto him, taking what he offered, giving what he had not yet asked for. Feelings were all, yet sensations were more. And they moved over her, in wave after dizzying wave.

Everything about him sang to her memory—his smell, the sounds of pleasure, of appreciation he made as he explored her body, the way he moved his tongue over hers, the texture of his hands as he slipped them under her gown and up her legs.

She sighed and arched her back as he plundered her neck with his mouth. His cheeks, rough with his morning beard, rasped against her skin, sending shivers over her. Her nipples hardened, aching to be touched.

He knew her needs without asking, without needing to be told. He brought his hands to her breasts, then his mouth. She longed for him to tear away her gown so she could feel his palms, his tongue against her naked flesh.

She curled her fingers into his hair, the golden strands crisp against her fingers. He brought his mouth to hers once more. She received it with a hunger, an aggressiveness that should have shocked her but didn't.

He was her husband; there would be a happy ending for them. She believed that; she had to.

Her skin was like warm silk. Royce tore his lips from hers, wanting to explore her softness with his eyes and mouth as well as his hands. He drew up to his knees, straddling her. It had been as long since he'd been able to feast his eyes on her as it had been his hands, and the wait had been an agony.

Now she was here and his; he wouldn't let this moment pass without basking in the luxury of just gazing at her. He roved his eyes over her, from the dark, alluring fan of her hair spread across the white pillow to her virginal high-necked gown. He met her gaze, at once sultry and shy. "You look part angel and part gypsy," he murmured, trailing his index finger over her dark eyebrow. "Which are you, Margaret Katherine Ryan? Angel or gypsy?"

"Just plain Maggie," she whispered, arching up as he trailed the same finger down and across her breasts.

"No." He shook his head. "Not plain." Slowly, not taking his gaze from her, he inched her gown up. "Exciting, tempting, infuriating." He lowered his eyes. "But never plain."

Maggie curled her fingers into the sheets, crumpling them, holding on for dear life. The feel of the satin gown brushing against her skin was unbelievably erotic. But even more erotic was the way he worshiped each morsel of her flesh as he exposed it—with his hands and mouth and eyes.

Royce loosened the ties at the neck of her gown, slipped it over her head and tossed the garment aside. He caught his breath at her beauty, then lifted his eyes once more to hers. "You are exquisite."

Not taking his gaze from hers, Royce ran the flat of his hands from her shoulders to her abdomen, stopping before he touched the most secret, most sensitive part of her. Her skin seemed hotter now, rosier even than Manda's had been earlier; her cheeks were wild with color.

"Do you remember?" he asked softly, his voice thick with desire.

"Everything..." Her breath shuddered past her lips as he moved his thumbs, brushing them ever so softly over the curls at the apex of her thighs. She fought the urge to grab his hands and place them where she needed them most. The fight left her panting. "I remember everything."

"This?" He traced his fingertips along the inside of her thigh, writing an invisible message.

She knew the game. It had been a silliness they'd invented when first married, as a way to prolong their lovemaking. Guessing right was rewarded with pleasure, wrong with the agony of waiting.

He moved his fingers again, and she arched up to meet them. "Oh, no," he whispered against her ear, drawing his hand away. "You know the rules... Concentrate, Maggie."

He moved his fingers over her again, titillating, teasing.

She bit back a moan. "Your name."

He sank his fingers into her, and she gasped and arched up to meet him. He pleasured her until she could stand no more, and she tangled her fingers in his hair, bringing his face up to meet hers.

"What do you want?" he whispered hoarsely. "Tell me, Maggie."

Everything, she wanted to shout. What we had... and lost. I want you without reservations or doubts. I want you and me and happily ever after.

But she said none of those things; they would only make him run.

Wrapping her legs around his, she undulated her hips, stroking and teasing, dodging when he made a move to claim her. This time it was his breath that shuddered out, his heart that thundered.

"I want you," she answered finally, panting from the effort of denial. "All of you. Now."

He tangled his hands in her hair; she in his. He moved inside her; she moved with him. Slow, gently at first, then faster, more fiercely.

Still they gazed at one another.

Maggie stripped away each of her guards, laying her gaze naked for him. She wanted him to see each of her hopes and fears, her longing and her love. She wanted him to read everything in her eyes.

But he lowered his gaze to her mouth, his lips to hers. She wanted to cry out her hurt, her distress. Either he couldn't see or wouldn't—one hurt as much as the other.

A moment later thinking became an impossibility, as did wishing or regretting. Sensations skyrocketed through her, and the sound of his name on her lips and hers on his reverberated through her head.

The trip back to reality, to evening breaths and slowing hearts, was gentle. Gradually Maggie's awareness grew to include more than Royce and her own body. She became aware of the sound of the grandfather clock chiming below, of the glow of dawn on the horizon, the rustle of the sheets. And her worries about what he thought, and more, what he felt.

Maggie drew in a deep breath and pushed her fears aside. She would worry, would face her feelings and Royce's another time. Now was too special, too perfect, to let slip away. Or worse, to waste.

She rubbed her mouth against his, then nipped its corner. She smiled, then giggled sleepily.

Royce arched his eyebrows even as he stroked her hair. ''Maggie, after a man has just…performed, the

last thing he hopes to hear is a very amused, very
feminine little snicker.''

She tipped her head back and laughed up at him.
''You were wonderful. Fabulous. A real stallion.''

He rubbed some of the silky midnight strands between his fingers. ''That's more like it.''

She fitted her cheek against his shoulder, stifling a
yawn. ''Actually, I was thinking of something Louise
once said.''

''There goes my self-confidence again.''

She bit back another yawn. ''It has to do with
making love.''

''Better.'' He propped himself on an elbow, and
amused, gazed down at her sleepy, satisfied face. ''But
I am curious. Want to fill me in?''

''Mmm...'' Maggie stretched sinuously. ''After
each of her babies came, she said sex was the last thing
on her mind for a long time. She said it was as if in one
fell swoop she'd gone from being a woman to a
mother.''

''Poor Joe.'' Royce leaned down and rubbed his
nose against hers. ''You have a point here?''

''Mmm, hmm.'' Maggie slipped her hands around
his neck. ''Making love has been the only thing on my
mind. For weeks.''

''Really?'' He arched his eyebrows in exaggerated
surprise. ''I haven't thought about it once.''

''Liar.'' She laughed and pressed her lips to the
pulse throbbing in his neck. ''You smell like me.''

''Do I?'' Her words brought the oddest sensation—part possessiveness, part blind terror.

"Mmm..." Maggie's eyes drooped. "I...like it."

"You need to get some sleep. It's almost dawn."

She shook her head, snuggling against him. "Almost...Christmas...Eve..." And then she was too sleepy to say more.

Royce was gone when Maggie awoke. He'd left a note saying he had an early meeting with a vendor and would be at Sassy's all day, but would be home in plenty of time for dinner. He hated to leave her, but she'd been sleeping so soundly he hated to wake her more. He also said that if anything happened at the pediatrician's, or if she needed him for any reason, she shouldn't hesitate to call.

Maggie clutched the note to her chest, her eyes filling with tears. He would be home for dinner; he'd told her to call if she needed him. He might not have consciously come to the decision, but he'd given her another chance. She knew it with her heart.

This time she wouldn't let their happiness slip away.

Laughing out loud, she flopped back against the pillows. This Christmas was going to be the most magical one ever. She and Royce were back together, Amanda and Alice would be with them. It would be a real family Christmas.

Feeling eighteen years old and buoyant enough to float through the rest of the day, Maggie bounded out of bed and went to check on Amanda. She still slept, but fitfully now. Maggie hurried and dressed, then called the pediatrician to make an appointment for her.

Maggie took her in; the physician confirmed her phone diagnosis and prescribed antibiotics. She also reassured Maggie that she hadn't done anything wrong and that there was no reason she and Mr. Adler shouldn't be able to enjoy the holidays as long as Amanda didn't become overtired or feverish again.

Comforted by the physician's words, Maggie turned her thoughts to less urgent, but still unsettling matters.

Tomorrow was Christmas and she had a million things left to do. And at the top of the list was a gift for Royce.

After getting Manda's prescription filled, Maggie stopped at her mother's on the chance she would be home and available for some last-minute baby-sitting.

"Mom," she called, sticking her head just inside her parents' front door. Christmas carols played softly in the background and the house smelled of a delicious blend of holiday cooking, evergreen and the unassuming floral scent her mother had always worn.

Maggie smiled. This was the kind of home she wanted to make for Amanda—one filled with warmth and laughter. She wanted her daughter to someday experience the same rush of love and security she did every time she came home.

Maggie looked down at her daughter. "Come on, sweetie," she murmured. "Let's go find Grandma."

The infant gurgled and Maggie laughed. "You're absolutely right, we should check the kitchen first."

Her mother was there, up to her elbows in oyster dressing and humming "Jingle Bells" under her breath.

"Hi, Mom."

Her mother whirled around, startled. "Maggie!"

"The door was open." Maggie made a clucking sound with her tongue and crossed the kitchen. She kissed her mother's cheek.

Eileen Ryan shook her head. "Josie must have forgotten to lock it. I had her run to the market for a few things. Have a seat."

"Thanks." Maggie snitched two snickerdoodles from the cookie tray, then sank onto one of the old ladder-back chairs set around the huge oak table. The chair creaked as she sank onto it; the tabletop was scarred from years of children's milk glasses and school projects. "She's off for the holidays?"

"Mmm, hmm." Eileen made a silly face at Amanda. "That university gives them a whole month off. Can you imagine?"

"Sounds good to me." Maggie propped Amanda into a sitting position on her lap, then dug in the diaper bag for a rattle. She pulled it out and handed it to Manda, who immediately stuck it in her mouth.

"What brings you here today?" her mother asked, turning back to the bowl of stuffing. "Did you come just to chitchat?"

"Or did I need a favor?" Maggie laughed, and Manda shook the rattle vigorously. "I did need a favor, but I hate to ask now that I see you're so busy."

"Nonsense," her mother said crisply. "Ask away."

Maggie told her mother about Amanda's ear infection and her frightening fever of the night before. "And I still need to pick up a few things for Christmas and stop at the grocery," she finished. "The stores are sure to be mobbed, and I hate to take Manda out when she's—"

"Say no more." Eileen scraped the sticky stuffing off her hands, then washed and dried them. She held out her arms. "I would love to watch my grandbaby for a few hours."

"If you're sure . . ."

"Positive. Josie said just this morning that she hadn't seen Manda in too long. And I'm way ahead of schedule."

"As usual." Maggie kissed Manda and placed her in her grandmother's arms. "I can't thank you enough, Mom."

"For doing what I love most? Fiddle." Her mother waved her toward the front door. "Go on, Manda and I are going to have a great time. Aren't we, baby?"

After promising to be back soon and assuring her mother that as it stood she and Royce would still be able to come for Christmas dinner, she hurried to the mall.

The stores were packed. Apparently the rest of New Orleans also had last-minute gifts to buy. But even though each stop took three times as long to complete as it normally would have, she enjoyed the crowds and the frenzied energy that crackled in the air.

She rushed from store to store, having no idea what to get Royce. She wanted to buy him everything; she

saw dozens of things she knew he'd like. But she had
to be judicious about this and only give him one or
two perfect things—he would feel overwhelmed by
anything else.

But perfect turned out to be damn difficult to decide on. She wanted something personal but not pres-
suring, caring but not overbearingly gushy. And
whatever she chose had to be reasonably inexpensive;
Royce would feel obligated by anything else.

She looked at robes and sweaters and belts.
Too... nondescript. She considered briefcases and
watches and art. Too... too...

Then she found it. Royce collected antique toys;
she'd bought him several really special ones over the
years they'd been together. And there in the window
of a bookstore was a large, lushly photographed book
on that very thing. Thank God.

She also bought him a huge box of his favorite Go-
diva chocolate cordials, then left the mall and headed
to the grocery. More of a madhouse than the mall—
New Orleanians did have their priorities—by the time
she'd shopped and picked Manda up, nearly three
hours had passed. By the time she got home, the afternoon was nearly gone.

Royce had said he would be home in "plenty of time
for dinner." That could be any minute and she hadn't
even started dinner, let alone gotten herself cleaned up
and looking presentable.

Maggie shook her head and grinned. Presentable?
No way. She wanted to be alluring; she wanted to
knock his socks off. And that took time.

"Where have you been?" Alice asked as Maggie stepped through the front door, juggling both the sleeping Amanda and several bags of groceries.

"Shopping," Maggie answered, out of breath. "There's more in the car." She dumped the bags and started for the stairs with Amanda. "I'm going to put Manda down. Josie and Mom wore her out—she slept all the way across the causeway."

By the time she came back downstairs, Alice had retrieved the rest of the groceries from the car and the bags were stacked on the kitchen counter.

Maggie began unpacking the bags, humming under her breath. "You should have seen the stores, Alice. They were a zoo and the traffic was even worse. Two women got in a fight at the grocery over the last bag of cranberries, and I saw three accidents on the way home. Tis the season, I guess."

"You didn't leave a note."

Maggie looked up from the groceries. "Pardon me?"

"A note," Alice repeated. "I didn't know where you were."

"Oh, I'm sorry, Alice. Truthfully, it never even occurred to me. I took Amanda to the doctor early, then dropped her at Mom's so I could do my last-minute shopping. I never thought I'd be gone so long." She shook her head. "It really was wild."

Maggie opened the fridge and started placing items inside. "Did you see all the goodies my mother sent? There's even a pecan pie. By the New Year, we'll all be too fat to fit into our clothes." She laughed as she opened the cheese keeper. "I'm usually the guilty party when it comes to loading everyone down with sweets, but with everything going on I didn't do any baking this year."

"I wish I could have gone with you." Alice stubbed the toe of her tennis shoe against the tile floor. "I hardly ever get to go into the city anymore."

Maggie frowned a little as she stuffed all the plastic bags into one, then put them in the bin to go to the recycling center. "I left early... and I knew you were working until one. We'll do it another time, Alice. I promise."

"Sure." She stubbed her toe against the floor once more. "It was slow at the coffeehouse."

"I thought it would be, because of the holiday." Maggie tossed a bag she'd missed in the bin. "Flip on the radio, will you? See if you can find some carols."

"Okay." Alice fiddled with it until she found some, then turned back to Maggie. "Dana split early."

"Could you give me a hand with the potatoes? The peeler's in the drawer next to the sink."

Alice slid open the drawer and took out the gadget. "What are you making?"

"Meat loaf and mashed potatoes."

Alice wrinkled her nose. "Not very Christmassy."

"Don't worry, you'll get the works tomorrow at my mother's. She makes more food than an army could eat." Maggie took a large bowl from a bottom cabinet. "You're really in for a treat. I hope you're still coming?"

"Yeah. Where else would I go?"

Maggie dumped the ground meat into the bowl and started adding spices. "Royce eats so much fancy food, he always enjoyed my plain cooking. Meat loaf and casseroles, you know, things like that. The stuff most men loathe." She laughed. "It's a good thing, too. I may be a whiz at baking, but when it comes to everything else, I'm pretty average—"

"What does *he* have to do with this?"

Maggie stopped and turned toward Alice. One look at her face and Maggie's stomach crashed to her toes. The look on her own face must have been telling, because Alice narrowed her eyes.

"So that's what this is all about," she sneered, folding her arms across her chest. "I wondered why you were acting so...out of breath and so...goofy. Singing and laughing and going on about nothing."

Maggie held out a hand to Alice, heat stinging her cheeks. "We need to talk."

The girl jutted her chin out. "You told me you two weren't getting back together."

"This situation is more complicated than that." Maggie pulled out a chair. "Sit down, Alice. Let's discuss it."

"What's the use? When we talk you don't tell me the truth."

"That's not fair." Maggie took a step toward the teenager. "When I told you that Royce and I weren't getting back together, I meant it. I never thought we might have a second chance. Never. But things have changed—"

"Yeah, you're right. Things sure have changed." Alice yanked on her denim jacket. "I'm out of here."

Maggie started after her. "Alice, wait! It's Christmas Eve. Can't we talk about this like two—"

The girl slammed the door in her face and ran down the walk toward the coffeehouse.

"Adults," Maggie finished, watching her go, a sinking sensation in the pit of her stomach.

When the girl disappeared from sight, she shut the door, then leaned against it. Dammit. Alice wasn't an adult. She was a hurting seventeen-year-old girl. She should have anticipated Alice's reaction to her and Royce getting back together; she should have planned to sit down with her to talk, to explain.

Maggie rested her head back against the door and looked up at the ceiling. She cringed as she recalled the tone of Alice's voice as she'd called her behavior silly, pictured her expression as she'd raced out the door.

In Maggie's joy over her and Royce's second chance, she'd forgotten all about Alice.

Her excitement of earlier did seem silly now, juvenile even. Her desire to make Royce his favorite meal, sillier still. The last thing she'd wanted to do was hurt Alice, but that was exactly what she'd done. It made her ache to think the girl might have lost trust in her.

She pushed away from the door and went back to work on the meat loaf, fighting back the tears that welled in her eyes. It was Christmas Eve, Maggie told herself. Alice would cool off, then come back. She would talk to her then. Everything would be all right.

Sure. Royce would be home soon, they would all have a wonderful evening together. Royce would build a fire, she would turn on the tree and they would all sit around it with a cup of eggnog. They would sing some Christmas carols and poke through the gifts when they thought no one was watching them.

It would be a scene right out of a Norman Rockwell painting.

Her eyes welled with tears again and, feeling more than a bit ridiculous, Maggie started to peel the potatoes.

Chapter Nine

"Merry Christmas, Honoria." Royce placed a small, elegantly wrapped gift on his sister's desk in front of her.

Honoria picked up the package and smiled. "You shouldn't have."

"I know." Royce perched on the edge of her desk, feeling ridiculously happy. "But if I hadn't you would have had my head."

"True." His sister shook the box, then expertly weighed it in her palm. "Hmm..."

"Curious?"

"Very." She set the package aside and arched her eyebrows speculatively. "You're awfully cheerful."

"It's Christmas." He nudged the box back in front of her with his forefinger. "Go ahead and open it."

"You know I always wait until Christmas morning."

"Make an exception." He grinned and inched the box a little closer to her. "I won't see you again until after you get back from Aspen."

She looked up at him, a question in her eyes, then shrugged. A moment later she peeled away the last of the foil wrapping and lifted the lid off the box. "Oh, Royce..." She held up the antique marcasite-and-pearl bar pin. "It's lovely. You've outdone yourself this year."

He helped her fasten it at her collar, enjoying the way she preened over her reflection in the small mirror she kept by her desk. Honoria rarely revealed her feelings, even in such a small way. "I'm glad you like it."

"I really do." She touched it one last time, then put the mirror aside. "I'd planned to bring your gift to Mother and Dad's tonight. You will be there?"

His parents' annual Christmas Eve open house. His smile slipped a bit. How could he have forgotten?

Maggie. That was how. And the incredible, exhausting and exhilarating night they'd had.

"I thought I'd skip it this year," he murmured nonchalantly, thumbing through a stack of her holiday greetings. "They're such mob scenes. I doubt they'll even miss me. Their guest list grows bigger and more important each year." He pulled a card from the stack. "Bitsy Billings? Is her brother still pining for you?"

Honoria tilted her head. "You have something more exciting planned tonight?"

Royce groaned silently. He'd told Honoria about Maggie's request that he move back in with her. He'd told her about the baby—Maggie's baby—offering the information in a factual no-nonsense manner.

But things had changed since he'd had that discussion with her, and there wasn't much his sister didn't see, especially when it came to him. Honoria had a mind like a steel trap and a heart to match.

"No." He slipped the card back into the stack. "But I'm tired. And it's Christmas Eve. Spending it at Mother and Dad's with two hundred of their nearest, dearest and most influential is my idea of Christmas hell."

"I see." Honoria took a cigarette from her case and tapped it against the desktop for a moment before lighting it. She inhaled, then blew a long stream of smoke toward the ceiling. She met his eyes again. "So, who are you going to spend the...night with, instead?"

"You have a point here?" Royce picked up her gold-plated lighter and slapped it against his palm, suddenly and unreasonably annoyed.

Honoria leaned back in her big upholstered chair and considered him thoughtfully through the haze of cigarette smoke. "A tad testy about this, aren't we?"

"And I asked, what's your point?"

She opened her mouth as if to respond, then shut it and shrugged. "No point, little brother."

He tossed down the lighter. "You might as well say what's on your mind, Honoria. You've never been one to hold back, and I don't see any reason to start now."

"Fine." She stubbed out the almost untouched cigarette. "Your working hours of late have been erratic. As has been your behavior. Ever since you moved back in with Maggie."

He narrowed his eyes. He knew exactly what she was getting at and it infuriated him. "And?"

"I'd hate to see you lose focus of what's important. That's all. I'd hate to see what happened last time happen again."

He stood. "You don't have to worry about me. I'm fine. Everything's under control."

"It is?"

"Yes, dammit. It is." He glared at her, knowing his very response testified to his lack of control right now.

She followed him to his feet. "Don't kid yourself, Royce. Mother and Dad will miss you tonight. Mother is an exceptionally good head counter."

He hated it when Honoria was right. And she was right about it all—he was expected to be at his parents', his absence would be noted...and when it came to Maggie, he'd completely lost his focus. Again.

He swore and checked his watch. Honoria smiled and smoothed a hand over her sleek blond bob. "So, little brother, should I bring your gift with me tonight?"

"Don't be so smug, sister dear." Royce kissed her cheek, grinning despite his annoyance. "It's unbecoming on a woman of your advanced age."

He left the office to the sound of her amusement.

His parents' open house was crowded, loud and as annoying as he'd feared it would be. Royce rubbed his throbbing temples. His parents had hired a jazz combo to play, and his head had begun to pound the moment he cleared the front door.

Frowning, Royce circled the room with his gaze, looking for whom or what he didn't know. His Aunt Prissy breezed by, sparing him hardly a glance; after all, he was only family, and she was hot on the trail of the society editor from the *Times-Picayune.*

He helped himself to a cup of eggnog, then wandered through the crowd. His mother always contracted party specialists to create her extravaganzas. This year the theme must be "all that glitters," because every material the designers had chosen either sparkled, gleamed or glowed. Vivid red and green Mylar bows decorated the swags, tree and wreaths, silver glitter had been sprinkled everywhere. Even the natural evergreen had been flocked with it.

Royce tipped his face toward the ceiling. Tiny white lights had been draped from the ceilings to capture, he suspected, the feeling of sparkling canopies of snow. No doubt the artists had envisioned creating a winter wonderland; he felt as if he'd gotten caught in a Macy's display window gone bad.

He looked around the room again, wishing the combo would at least attempt a rendition of "Jingle Bells" or "Deck the Halls." And wishing he were home.

Home. He shook his head and took a sip of his eggnog. In a way that was exactly where he was. This was the house he'd grown up in, the kind of parties, the people he'd grown up around. But he didn't feel "at home," didn't feel comfortable.

"You're late."

At the sound of his mother's cultured voice, he turned slowly and faced her. Trim, elegant, coolly beautiful, his mother had been one of the reigning queens of New Orleans society since she'd married his father nearly forty years ago. "Mother." He kissed her cheek. "You look lovely."

She ran a hand down her emerald-colored velvet shift. "It is rather nice, isn't it? Jacques designed it for me."

"And the necklace?"

She lifted her hand to the blaze of emeralds and diamonds at her throat. "Your father's Christmas gift to me. I picked it out myself."

Royce looked away. How many years had they been married, he wondered, before his mother had begun choosing her own Christmas presents? She'd been doing it for as long as he could remember. "Where is he?"

"Here someplace." She laid a hand on his arm. "Be sure to wish Senators Blake and Martin a happy holiday. And when you speak to the mayor, be sure to express dissatisfaction over that Orleans Parish business tax he's proposing. Honestly, I get so weary of paying for those who refuse to pull their own weight.''

Royce lowered his eyes to her necklace, then lifted them back to hers. "I'm sure you do, Mother."

She swept her gaze over him, pausing at his loosened tie. "Honoria's been telling me some disturbing things about you."

"Oh?" He arched an eyebrow in question, although he had no doubt to what she referred.

"She tells me you and that . . . Maggie are living together again?"

"That Maggie?" he repeated carefully, controlling the flash of fury. "Certainly you're not referring to my wife?"

"So, it's true?"

"It's true."

"I see."

Royce thought of Maggie, of her warmth, of the way he felt when she was in his arms. "Do you, Mother?"

"I thought it was over."

"You thought wrong."

She smiled coolly. He recognized that particular curving of her lips from many of the momentous occasions of his life, including the evening he and Maggie had announced their engagement.

He took a step closer; he lowered his voice. "And did Honoria tell you you're a grandmother?"

Color flooded her cheeks. "That's Maggie's baby."

Royce paused. *Maggie's baby*. Something about the words and the way she said them rankled. He stiffened. "Her name's Amanda, Mother."

She made a sound of annoyance. "I suppose it would have been too much to ask for you to discuss this with..." She shook her head. "Never mind. I never could control you."

Royce drained his eggnog. "Control is such an ugly word."

"You know what I meant."

He looked her straight in the eye. "Yes, I do."

She stepped back, flustered. "You're not yourself tonight, Royce. Have a glass of champagne."

She started to move off; he stopped her with a hand to her elbow. She met his eyes. He smiled. "Merry Christmas, Mother."

Color flooded her cheeks. "Merry...Christmas to you, too."

She turned and was swallowed by the crowd.

"You can leave now," Honoria whispered, coming up behind him. "Your head's been counted."

He turned and grinned at her. "You've been gossiping about me."

"Mother and I have to have something to talk about." She caught his arm. "Come into the library with me. There's something I want to show you."

They slipped through the throng of partiers and into the library. There, he turned to his sister. "You look like the proverbial canary."

She held out her hand. "Brian's Christmas present."

The third finger on her left hand sported a diamond solitaire of at least five carats. Royce looked from it to his sister. "Why are you doing this?"

She frowned. "What a question."

"A good question, Honoria. I didn't think you were that fond of him. Certainly not this fond."

She snatched her hand back. "I thought you would be happy for me."

"I would be if you really wanted this. Two weeks ago you called him a buffoon."

"Honestly, Royce!" She spun away from him and crossed to their father's desk. She flipped up the lid of the teak cigarette box, selected one and lit it. When she turned back to him, her eyes were glassy. "Why am I doing it? He's Brian Bennett III and I'm Honoria Adler. And neither one of us has any illusions about the other's motives."

He wasn't surprised by her news, not really. It shouldn't bother him a bit. He wanted to shake her silly, anyway.

Crossing to her, he cupped her face in his palms. As he gazed into her eyes he thought of his mother's word of minutes ago—control.

"Illusions aren't so bad," he murmured. "You've waited a long time, Honoria. Wait a little longer. Don't marry Brian because Mother and Dad—or anyone else for that matter—would think it a good match."

She jerked away from him. "You married for love. Where did it get you? Love isn't for people like us, Royce. I thought you'd figured that out."

Royce stared at her a moment, nonplussed. "Who said anything about love?" he asked quietly. "I don't remember using that word."

Honoria stubbed out the cigarette; he saw that her hand shook. When she looked back at him, her mask of composure had slipped firmly back into place. "Are you going to wish me well?" she asked coolly. "Or not?"

"I always wish you well. You're my sister. I just wish..." He let his words trail off, leaned over and kissed her cheeks. "Congratulations, Honoria. You will make a stunning bride."

Many hours later he let himself into the house he shared with Maggie. As he stepped through the front door he became aware of the smell of the fire and of the hum of Christmas carols. How different from the cacophony of sounds and exotic smells of the house he'd just come from. And how much...warmer.

Home. He smiled, relaxation easing over and through him. He shrugged out of his coat and hung it up, then crossed to the parlor.

Maggie was there, singing to herself as she arranged packages under the tree. The lights on the tree twinkled; everywhere were touches of Christmas, from the stockings hung on the mantel to the dish of traditional holiday candies on the coffee table.

He leaned against the doorjamb, enjoying watching her, liking the sound of her off-key rendition of "Deck the Halls." She looked lovely, soft and flushed and totally kissable.

He trailed his gaze over her. She wore a forest green shawl-necked sweater and matching slacks, she'd draped a red-and-white scarf over her shoulders for a final festive touch. Gold gleamed at her ears, her hair streamed down her back in a riot of inky waves.

She should have been at the party, he thought, guilt pricking him. She should have been out with people, not home alone waiting for him.

Royce thought of the disappointment he'd heard in her voice when he called, had heard despite her attempt to hide it, and cursed under his breath as the guilt pricked again.

He shook off the emotion, just as he'd shaken off his confusion at his feelings about Honoria's announcement and his parents' jubilant reaction to it. He had done nothing to feel guilty about; he and Maggie had made no promises to each other. Last night had just...happened. They were, after all, still married. They had needs and had always been attracted to—

She looked up and caught him watching her and smiled. "You're home."

The curving of her lips was immediate and welcoming; it warmed him clear to his core. He smiled back. "You look beautiful."

She flushed. "Thanks."

"I brought you these." He held out a small baker's box and a bottle of champagne. "The champagne's good. Mother and Dad's private stock. I had the caterer put together an assortment of canapés, since you couldn't be there to enjoy them."

"Thanks," she murmured hesitantly, taking what he offered. "Are you hungry? I saved you dinner."

Royce saw the hurt come and go in her eyes and swore silently. He hadn't done anything wrong, he told himself again fiercely. "Starved. You know I can't fill up on finger food."

"Good." She clasped her hands in front of her. "If you want to change, I'll fix you a plate."

"Great. I'll be right back."

Maggie watched him go, doubts racing over her. Dear Lord, she loved him so much she felt as if she might burst from it. If only she could be sure of his feelings, if only she knew for certain that he wanted them to try again.

She frowned and started for the kitchen. He hadn't asked her to join him at the party. In the hours since he called to tell her he was going to be late, she'd told herself she couldn't have gone anyway, because of Amanda. She told herself that was why he hadn't asked.

But she couldn't keep herself from thinking that he hadn't wanted her at his parents', that he wasn't ready to do more than play house with her.

She pushed her insecurities away and called herself an idiot. This situation was as uncertain, as fragile as the first blossoms of spring. Royce had never been good at dealing with emotions, especially when they were his own. He thought himself a man of reason, thought himself a rock. She knew better. He was a man of great emotion...just one who was uncomfortable with it.

She uncovered the plate she'd fixed him earlier and popped it in the microwave. He was here, wasn't he? He was being sweet—bringing her wine and hors d'oeuvres from the party. She had to give this some time . . . had to give him some time.

"It smells wonderful."

Maggie turned and met his eyes, searching his expression. In that moment, as he steadily returned her gaze, she wondered if she should just go ahead and tell him she loved him. Tell him and beg for another chance.

Good God, what if she did and he walked?

"Maggie, are you all right?"

She nodded and forced herself to smile. "Fine." She turned back to the counter and his plate, willing her hands to steady.

He crossed the room, stopping behind her and peeking over her shoulder. "Is that your famous meat loaf?"

"It is." She looked back at him, trying to appear relaxed, but the flutter of butterflies in her stomach made it impossible. He was so close she could see the flecks of green in his blue eyes, feel his breath against her cheek, feel the heat that emanated from him. If she moved just a fraction, her shoulders would brush against his chest.

She drew a deep breath and steeled herself against doing just that. "It's something you always liked—" her words faltered, and she cleared her throat "—but it might be a little dried out by now."

"I'm sure—" he murmured, his voice thick, his eyes lowering to her mouth "—it'll be wonderful."

Heat flooded her cheeks . . . and every other part of her body. "I hope so."

He took the plate from her hands and set it on the table. She followed with a small plate of the canapés, setting it at an adjoining place.

She perched on the chair kitty-corner to his. He'd exchanged his suit and tie for soft black jeans and a gold cashmere sweater. Maggie caught herself staring at the vee of muscled chest exposed by the sweater's neck and jerked her gaze back to his face.

"How was your day?" she asked quickly, hoping to mask her nervousness.

"Busy. How was yours?" He took a forkful of food.

"Busy." She nibbled on the corner of one of the hors d'oeuvres, then set it back down. They were married; this shouldn't be so awkward. She shouldn't be so on edge.

It shouldn't be so important that everything be perfect.

She cleared her throat again, searching for something to say. The only things she could think of had absolutely nothing to do with talking.

"How's Manda?"

"Better. Sleeping well." Maggie filled him in on the visit to the doctor, then silence fell between them again.

He made small talk, so did she. He took a few bites of food, she pushed the canapés around her plate. Minutes passed.

Finally, he set his fork down. "Maggie?"

She looked up. "Yes."

"I'm not really hungry."

"Neither am I."

"Why don't we pop the champagne and go sit by the tree?"

She smiled, relieved. "I'd love that."

A short while later they sat curled up on the floor, the oversize pillows bunched up around and behind them, their glasses filled with the sparkling wine.

Royce tapped her flute with his; the crystal pinged. "Merry Christmas, Maggie," he said softly.

At the heat in his gaze, her heartbeat tripled. "Merry Christmas, Royce."

She sipped. The wine was light and dry and fine. During the time she'd lived with Royce she had come to know the difference in quality of wines, and this was a good one.

"Your parents are going to miss this bottle," she murmured, taking another sip and enjoying the way the bubbles went to her head.

"Don't worry. They'll think the butler did it."

"They don't have a butler."

Royce laughed and leaned his head back against the pillow. "I'll send them a check tomorrow."

"Tomorrow's Christmas."

"So it is. I'll send one the day after, then." He turned his face to hers. "You look so beautiful tonight."

She flushed with pleasure. "You said that before."

"I can't say it enough."

She sucked in a deep breath. Good God, she felt like she might faint from wanting.

He smiled and looked away, toward the tree once more. "I see Santa's already come."

"You know how my family is." Maggie laughed lightly. "Most of them are for Amanda. Three months old and spoiled already."

Royce caught her hand and brought it to his mouth. "She deserves to be spoiled. She's a wonderful little girl."

Maggie couldn't help but think of Alice, another wonderful little girl who should have been spoiled, but instead had gotten worse than nothing. Maggie frowned. She hated having argued with her, especially on Christmas Eve.

"Maggie?" Royce touched the corner of her mouth with his index finger. "Is something wrong? Is there something you haven't told me about Manda—"

"No," Maggie said quickly. "It's Alice. We had an argument tonight. She stormed out."

"She's home now?"

"Yes." Maggie sighed and stared into her wine. "She wouldn't speak to me when she came back."

Royce caught her hand once more and rubbed his thumb across her knuckles. "What was the argument about?"

Maggie started to tell him, then stopped. What could she say? *We argued about you and me getting back together?* Hardly.

She shook her head. "Nothing. It'll be fine."

He brought her hand to his mouth and brushed his lips across the path his thumb had just taken. "You're sure?"

"I'm sure."

"Good." He took her champagne glass and set it by his. "Because I prefer not to talk at all anymore."

"No?"

"No." He pressed his lips to her palm. She shuddered and closed her eyes. "And I don't want your mind on anything but me. Come here, Maggie."

He gathered her to him and eased her back against the pillows. He cupped her face in his palms. "I've wanted to do this all day."

"Have you?" she whispered.

"Mmm, hmm." He brushed his mouth ever so softly against hers; it trembled under his. "But that's not the only thing I wanted to do."

"No?" She looped her arms around his neck, breathless and aching already.

He moved his mouth across her cheek to the side of her neck. He found the pulse that beat wildly there and pressed his lips to the spot. She sighed and arched her back.

"Uh-uh." He untied her silky scarf and slid it off, then nudged aside the neck of her sweater. She murmured her pleasure as his lips moved over the curve of her shoulder, then to the swell of her breast.

She closed her eyes, arching again as he skimmed his hands under the sweater, finding her breasts and cupping them through her lacy brassiere.

"You're wearing too many clothes, Maggie," he murmured, smiling against her mouth.

"So are you." She mimicked him, running the flat of her hands under his sweater. His skin was firm and hot under her fingers, his heartbeat sure but not steady beneath her palm.

He caught her lips, her tongue, in a long, breath-stealing kiss, then pulled away. "What are we going to do about this problem?"

"I have some ideas." Maggie lowered her hands to the waistband of his jeans.

He caught her fingers. "Hold that thought," he whispered. "I'll be right back."

She watched as he crossed to the parlor doors, closed and locked them. On his way back, he grabbed Amanda's play quilt from the back of the sofa. He lowered himself to the floor once more.

"Thank you."

"For what?"

She smiled and rubbed her nose against his. "For being so thoughtful."

He laughed huskily and rolled so that he lay partially on top of her. "Pure selfishness. I don't want to chance an interruption. I have big plans for us. Now—" he rotated his hips against hers "—where were we?"

"Right here," Maggie whispered, and slowly lowered his zipper.

Chapter Ten

The rest of the evening passed in a kaleidoscope of sensual delight. Royce pleasured her and she him, touching, exploring, reinventing themselves. When one could stand no more, the other would return the favor, not stopping until they cried out for release.

Sometime during the night, Royce swept her into his arms and carried her up to their bed. There, they made love again, slowly, deliciously.

Sleep came immediately after, a deep sleep filled with Royce and dreams of happily ever after.

The next morning Santa came late. Blessedly late. Amanda slept in and Alice...well, Alice was a teen-ager, after all.

Maggie and Royce lay on their sides on the big bed, totally nude, facing one another. He ran a finger over her lips. "I have a surprise for you."

Maggie smiled, exhausted from their lovemaking, but delectably so. "You do?"

"Mmm, hmm."

She moved against him, delighted to discover he was hard for her already...again. She trailed her fingertips across his chest. "Funny, I didn't see you come in with any packages last night."

"Maybe my surprise is right here." He wiggled his eyebrows. "Look under the blanket, my dear. I have a present for you."

Maggie peeked underneath, then back up at him, eyes wide with mock innocence. "You must be mistaken, sir, there's nothing under here I'd want."

Royce laughed and dragged her back up until they lay face-to-face once again. "You must be Maggie's evil twin sister. What have you done with the sweet, agreeable girl I went to bed with last night?"

"It's Christmas and she wants her present." Maggie pouted playfully. "And if you didn't get me one, I'm going to pinch you silly."

"Oh, yeah?" He caught her hands and brought them over her head. "You and who else?"

"My evil twin."

"Sounds kinky." He trailed his mouth across her breasts.

"Royce!" She squirmed. "Let me go."

He laughed. "Do that again, that was fun."

She glared up at him. "Did you get me a present?"

"Yes."

"Did you get me more than one?"

"Yes."

"Where are they?"

"Where they're supposed to be. Under the tree."

"Then it's time to get up."

"Is that greed I see gleaming in your eyes?"

"You bet." He released her hands, and she rolled out of bed. "Come on, lazy. It's time to get up."

Royce lay back against the pillows, grinning. "I already am."

"You . . . you're . . ." She wagged a finger at him. "Think about this, slug puppy. If you don't get up, Alice, Amanda and I will open your presents for you. Then we'll take them back for store credits."

That did the trick, because not long after that everybody, including Royce, had pulled themselves out of bed, dressed decently enough for each other's company and gathered around the Christmas tree.

Maggie made them all hot chocolate topped with real whipped cream, and while they opened their packages they drank the chocolate and ate her mother's Christmas cookies. Even Alice seemed to forget her anger of the night before and got into the spirit of the day.

If she'd had any doubts about Royce's feelings, they evaporated as the minutes ticked past. He'd bought her the sweetest, most thoughtful gifts—some silly woolly socks because her feet were always cold, a pound of her favorite treat in the whole world—spiced, candied cashews from a shop in the French

Quarter, and the sweetest gift of all, he'd arranged with a florist to have fresh flowers delivered every Monday until spring when the azaleas would be in full bloom once again.

His gift to Alice was just as thoughtful. He'd gotten her a cloisonné pendant of a butterfly breaking out of its cocoon and into flight. Her eyes suspiciously bright, she fastened it around her neck, then fished under the tree for a package she'd placed there for Royce.

She handed him the gift almost shyly and smiling; he tore it open. She'd given him a pamphlet of coffee facts and several sample packages of flavored coffees she'd combined herself. He seemed as surprised—and pleased—by her gesture as she'd been by his.

When he finally got to her big present, Maggie held her breath. He peeled the paper away, then for long moments stared at the book. She knew he loved it by the way he leafed through it, turning the pages almost reverently. And by the way he thanked her—with a kiss so tender it brought tears to her eyes.

Once their gifts were all opened, they scattered to get cleaned up and ready to go to her parents. There, too, the hours passed happily and without hint of stress. They feasted on the traditional holiday fare as well as some New Orleans favorites such as seafood-stuffed bell peppers and dirty rice. After the meal they all sat around the tree and talked about the past year and the upcoming year. It was a perfect, magical day. Maggie had never been happier.

* * *

The entire holiday season and the weeks following the New Year had seemed touched by the magic of Christmas Day.

Maggie bent her head to the bouquet of exquisite winter blossoms, breathing in their light but heady scent. She smiled softly. Monday again. The fourth since Christmas.

She took one last whiff of the flowers, then turned away from them and crossed to the parlor's picture window. Royce was outside with Manda, giving her a walking tour of the yard.

Maggie watched them. The scene should have warmed her, should have filled her with hope. Instead, a strange trembling started in the pit of her stomach and her smile faded.

Something was not right.

She shook her head. Nonsense. She was being paranoid, letting her insecurities and her imagination run away with her. Royce had played the attentive, loving husband. Over the past weeks, they'd gone to shows and dinner and had taken Amanda to the...

Played.

Maggie stopped on her own description, then shook her head again. Ridiculous. Everything was wonderful.

Perfect. They made love every morning and every night; they'd been unbelievably happy.

Unbelievably. Played.

Maggie turned away from the window, her frown deepening. She'd been happily married to Royce before; she knew when she had all of him. She knew what it was like to have his love.

This wasn't it.

The trembling spread until even her fingertips shook. She folded her arms across her chest. As often as she told herself that all was perfect, as often as she looked at her fresh flowers and reassured herself about Royce's feelings, the truth was, Royce was playing at this. He wasn't giving them another chance, he was only going through the motions.

She sucked in a deep breath. Dear Lord, how could she have been so wrong? How could she have been such a fool to believe—

Royce and Manda burst through the front door. Royce was laughing, Manda squealing. Maggie wanted to cry out in pain and frustration.

"You've got a real little genius here, Mags," he teased, unzipping Manda's jacket. "She knew each one of the plants by name. She could even spell them." Manda gurgled. "There, she did it again."

Maggie swung around and stared at him. An hour ago she would have laughed at his teasing, found hope in the fact that he enjoyed playing with Amanda. But an hour ago she still believed they had a chance, still believed wishes could come true.

Now all she could feel was betrayed. And all she could see was the cold, hard truth. "Don't you mean *we* have a genius?" she whispered, breathless and aching.

"Excuse me?"

He had no intention of being Amanda's father... not ever. Just another thing he was playing at. "Never mind. You don't."

Royce frowned and shrugged out of his jacket. "What's gotten into you? When Manda and I went outside twenty minutes ago you were all smiles."

She wanted to throttle him; she wanted to burst into tears. Instead, she said stiffly, "It's time for her bottle." Maggie took Amanda from him. "Excuse me."

Royce followed her into the kitchen. "What's the problem, Maggie?"

Maggie looked down at Manda's flushed and happy face and bit back her angry words. "I don't want to talk about it."

"I think you do. You're sure as hell acting like it."

"Not in front of Manda." Maggie yanked open the refrigerator and retrieved a bottle. After loosening the cap and putting the bottle in the microwave, she faced him again. "She might not be able to understand the words, but the emotions behind them she understands very well." The oven buzzed and Maggie took the bottle out and tightened the cap.

"Well, I hardly think this is fooling her," he muttered sarcastically, then swore. "I can't talk to you when you get like this."

"Get like what?" she asked, furiously. "Emotional?"

"Irrational."

"Damn you, Royce." Amanda began to whimper, and Maggie took a deep, calming breath. "I'm going to give Amanda her bottle, then put her down for her nap. If you're still around, we'll talk then.''

Royce swore again. "And where would I be, Maggie?"

She didn't answer him. Tears flooding her eyes, she fled the kitchen.

Nearly forty minutes later, Amanda asleep in her crib, Maggie tiptoed out of the nursery, closing the door softly behind her. She squeezed her eyes shut and said a quick prayer.

Showdown time.

She found Royce in the parlor, staring moodily out at the day. She could tell by the line of his back and shoulders that he was angry. Taking a deep breath, she stepped into the room. "We need to talk."

Royce turned and faced her, eyes narrowed. "You've got that right. What's with the Jekyll and Hyde routine?"

She inched her chin up. "Weeks ago I asked you what we were doing here, and you told me we were playing a game." She took another step toward him. "I need to know if anything's changed, or if you're still...playing."

He jammed his hands into his pockets. "What brought this on?"

"That doesn't answer my question, Royce. Maybe I better try a different approach." She moved farther into the room, head held high. "I love you."

A second turned into two, turned into a dozen. Regrets raced into his eyes; she swore silently and repeated herself. "I love you."

"No." He shook his head. "No, you don't."

Maggie held on to her calm. It took everything she had. She'd lost already, and she'd hardly begun. No, she vowed fiercely, she wouldn't give up so easily, she wouldn't be bowed.

"Yes, I do."

"Dammit." He turned to the window and knocked his fist against its frame. When he looked back at her she saw he was furious. "Why are you doing this, Maggie?"

"I don't have any ulterior motives. I only—"

"You said no promises. You said you didn't want anything from me."

"And you prefer that?" she shot back, working to control her temper, acknowledging the futility of even trying. "I love you and want another chance. I think we deserve another chance. What I need to know is if you think that's possible. Considering the circumstances, it's not too much to ask."

"When did this happen?" he demanded. "When did you decide all this? While I was out with Amanda?"

She cringed at his sarcasm but answered without tremor or hesitation. "The night we made love. This hasn't been about sex for me. But you know me well enough to know that already."

"Yeah, I know you well enough." He rubbed his hands over his face. "I don't believe this. I can't believe I fell for it. Again."

Her hands began to shake, and she folded them primly in front of her. "You want to tell me just what the hell you're thinking?"

He looked at her long and hard, not one whit of softness or compassion in his expression. "After that night when Amanda was so sick," he said slowly, his voice as tight as his expression, "you decided having a father for her wasn't such a bad idea. So you lured me into bed to remind me how it could be between us. That's what this has been about. This whole thing, from the very beginning, has been about your need for a father for Amanda."

"What!" She flew across the room, stopping close enough to touch him. Her legs shook so badly she wondered if they would support her. Jutting her chin out, she faced him. "First of all, I did not lure you into bed. I do not lure. Secondly, Amanda has nothing to do with my feelings for you. I never stopped loving you.... I only stopped believing in you and me."

"And you believe in us now?"

She held her ground even though the disbelief in his tone clawed at her. "Yes."

He laughed, the sound anything but amused. "Come off it, Maggie. You asked me to live with you so you could have Manda. You asked me to *pretend* to be the happy husband. Now you've had time to assess the situation and—"

"Assess the situation?" she repeated, folding her arms across her chest. "You make me sound like a cold-blooded schemer."

When he only lifted his eyebrows, her cheeks heated. "I told you I love you. That's the truth. I never stopped. Also truth."

"Love?" He practically spat the word back at her. "I don't believe in it... Not unfettered love, anyway. Not love without strings attached. And what about truth? If there was no Manda, would you still want me? Would you be standing here asking for another chance at our marriage?"

"That's not fair. She brought us back together. She made me see that you—"

"No, Maggie. Your machinations brought us back together. And the only thing she helped you see was that you needed a father for her."

His words should have torn at her, should have left her broken and weeping. A year ago they had, a month ago they still would have. She thought of the way he'd murmured her name every time they made love, of the way he cradled Manda in his arms, of the sweetness of his Christmas gifts, and she fought off her feelings of hopelessness and defeat.

She'd always thought of Royce as indestructible, totally confident and self-contained. She gazed at him now, seeing what she never had before—a vulnerable man, a man who needed affection, needed love. And one who was terrified of needing anything.

He wasn't rejecting her, she realized, he was running for dear life.

A calm settled over her, a determination. It could work between them, they could make it work. It was up to her to convince him.

She met and held his gaze. "What are you afraid of?"

Royce shook his head. "All these weeks now, you've been dishonest with me. I don't think we have anything to talk about."

He tried to walk away, but she caught his arm. "You're terrified of feeling too much. For me, for Manda. You say you don't believe in love.... That's the lie, Royce."

Something came into his eyes that renewed her, then it disappeared and he shrugged. "Whatever you need to believe, Maggie."

"What did you feel for me when we were first married, if not love?" she asked, catching his other hand. "Remember how happy we were? Remember the feeling, the want to be together every second of every day?"

"I wanted to believe in love," he said softly, tearing his gaze away from hers. "I made myself believe in it. I was a fool."

"You're a fool now." She dragged him to her. "We were happy once, we can be happy again."

"You have everything you wanted. A baby. Alice. And now you want me back. It's convenient, Maggie. Damn convenient."

"I've wanted you back all along." She slid her hands up his chest and circled his neck.

"We can't go back, Maggie. It's impossible." He took her hands from around his neck and set her away from him. "I'm giving you everything I'm able to give already. I can't love you."

"I don't believe you."

"Bulldozing again, Maggie? Just like when you didn't believe I might not want children?"

"It's not the same."

"It is."

"You're right, we can't go back. But we can go forward, Royce. Give us another chance." She caught him to her again. "Let's live together as husband and wife—for real this time. Let's try, really try. I know I can make it work, I know I can prove to you that I love you...that there are no strings attached to the way I feel. If after the adoption's final your feelings haven't changed, I'll let you go."

"Maggie, I—"

"No. Don't say anything else. Don't think, don't rationalize. Amanda is just over four months old, we have two more months together anyway." She slipped her hands around his neck and tangled her fingers in his hair. "Give us this time or—if you won't—at least let me believe that you are."

"Maggie...."

"No." She brought his head toward hers. "No talking. Just kiss me, Royce."

His pause lasted only a heartbeat, then he lowered his mouth to hers in a bruising kiss.

Chapter Eleven

Royce watched Maggie as she slept. Ten days had passed since their confrontation, and in that time he'd begun to wonder if she wasn't right. Maybe they could try again, maybe he felt more for her than he'd admitted to her. Or to himself.

Even as the thought filled his head, a knot of denial tightened in his chest. He breathed deeply, attempting to shake off the sensation. He didn't want to feel anything for her or Manda. But he did. That was the damnable part of it. Maybe it wasn't love, but it was strong. So strong it made him ache.

As did the thought of going on without her.

Royce roamed his gaze over her sleeping form. Her dark hair spilled across her pillow and onto his. He

caught some of the silky strands and rubbed them between his fingers, then brought them to his nose. They
smelled of her fruity shampoo and sunshine. They felt
like heaven against his skin.

He shook his head. He'd become a romantic. A
blithering starry-eyed romantic. And he'd been happy.
Incredibly, deliriously happy.

Royce frowned, not liking his own descriptions. He
let go of her hair and rolled onto his back and stared
up at the ceiling. Could he walk away from Maggie?
From Amanda and Alice? Could he just say goodbye? The thought brought a breathlessness and a
hunger. For Maggie's warmth, her laughter, for the
light that bathed his world when he was with her.

He didn't think he could let go. But that was what
he'd have to do. Maggie wouldn't settle for less than
everything. She'd made that clear.

Royce turned his head and looked at her again. And
what of Amanda? Having Maggie meant being
Amanda's father. *Dad,* he thought, testing the sound
of it in his head. *Daddy.*

He frowned, unsure of how the name sounded when
applied to him, unsure of how he felt about it. When
he and Maggie had talked about children, way back
before it had all fallen apart, those words had struck
him with fear. But then "children" had been in the
abstract. Amanda was real. She was here, a "now,"
not a "someday."

Royce drew his eyebrows together. She was an
adorable child. Beautiful and bright. She grew with

each day in so many ways. It had been magic to witness. He enjoyed her. He liked having her around.

Every time they'd taken her to the park, to a restaurant or the mall, people had stopped and commented on her. He felt awkward about the attention. But proud, too. And when they called him her father, he never corrected them.

Royce frowned again. But none of those feelings added up to the love and commitment necessary to be a father.

He closed his eyes and thought of the way her eyes searched for him when he walked into the room, of the way she waved and kicked and gurgled when he spoke to her...almost as if she were telling him all about her day and that she had missed him.

Royce shook his head. Ridiculous. She was a baby. She couldn't talk, couldn't intellectualize. He thought of the way she curled her fingers around one of his and held on, and of the way that made him feel, and he acknowledged that intellectualizing hadn't a damned thing to do with this.

But he also knew that with kids things couldn't be done in half measures. Kids couldn't be fooled, they understood feelings, tuned in to them. If he was going to be Amanda's father, he had to be him in every way. He had to be prepared to sacrifice for her. He had to love her.

He wouldn't be his parents.

Royce breathed deeply, a funny trembling sensation in the pit of his stomach. He rolled onto his back once more to stare up at the ceiling. Again it all came back to love. Was he capable?

He thought of his parents, of his relationship with Honoria, of those last months before he and Maggie split up, and sighed. He didn't know. He just didn't know.

"Stop that."

Royce turned his head. Maggie had awakened and was looking at him, love shining unabashedly from her eyes. What would it be like to feel as easily, as abundantly as Maggie did? To have so much to give?

"Stop," she repeated, reaching out and caressing his cheek. "Stop thinking so much."

He turned his head and kissed her fingertips. "You're amazing."

"I know." Maggie snuggled up to him. She moved her hands across his shoulders and chest, stroking down to his flat muscled belly and beyond. Laughing, she met his eyes. "So are you."

He groaned. "Come here." He pulled her to him, lifting her so she straddled him. Slowly he eased her onto his hardness.

She arched her back and moaned her pleasure. Curling her fingers into the hair on his chest, she began to move, rotating her hips, riding him, controlling their pleasure.

The sensation was incredible, but soon he could no longer remain passive. He caught her hips and guided her, moving faster until panting, they called out each other's names, and she collapsed against him.

"I may never walk upright again," she murmured against his shoulder.

He laughed and pushed the dampened tendrils of hair away from her face. "We could stay here forever."

"Mmm..." She stretched and yawned. "Speaking of which, what time do you have to go in to Sassy's?"

"Not until one."

She lifted her head and met his eyes. "Could you watch Manda for a couple of hours? I need to go over to the coffeehouse."

"Sure." He nuzzled her neck. "Problem?"

"No. I just need to check on things. It's been a while." She stretched again. "I'm thinking of going back to work. Not full-time, just a couple of hours a day. I'll bring Manda, put her in her playpen."

"Whatever you want to do."

"Right." Maggie rolled off him and sat up, pulling the sheet around her. "I need to get going. Amanda's going to howl for her bottle any moment."

He frowned, hearing the hurt in her voice. "Did I say something wrong?"

"Nothing." She scooted away. "Never mind."

"Oh, no." He crooked his finger at her. "Come back here. Talk to me."

She hesitated, then made a sound of frustration. "There's Amanda now."

Royce sat up. The infant had begun to stir in the other room, whimpering and gurgling to herself in her crib. He smiled a little, listening. She talked to her mobile and stuffed toys in the mornings, and when she grew tired of that she'd play with her feet for a minute or two. Only then did she howl for her bottle. It gave a body a chance to wake up and get a robe.

He looked back at Maggie. She was watching him, her expression tender. He cleared his throat, embarrassed. "You go ahead and get started. I'll get her bottle."

"Okay." Maggie leaned over and kissed him. "Thanks."

She slipped out of bed. He propped himself on an elbow and watched her as she arched her back and stretched, then slipped into her robe. God, she was beautiful. Sometimes just looking at her took his breath away. "How about lunch when you're done at the coffeehouse?"

She looked over her shoulder at him, surprised. "You'll have time?"

"I'll make time."

She smiled brilliantly. "I'd like that."

Several hours later they sat at a table on a wide, open veranda that faced the Tchefuncte River as it wound its way through the tiny town of Madisonville. Ceiling fans whirred quietly above, the sound of cutlery and conversation lulled as gently as the breeze.

"That was delicious. I haven't had an oyster po'boy in ages." She pushed her plate away. "Thank you."

"My pleasure," Royce murmured, watching Amanda. Maggie had placed her infant seat on the table, and Amanda batted at a soft, springy toy attached to the chair's side.

"It smells like spring," Maggie said, lifting her face to the sun and drawing in a lungful of the fresh air. "I can't believe another cold front's supposed to come through tonight."

"Even though it's still February it seems impossible, considering today." He took one of Amanda's rattles and touched her nose with it, then drew it away. The infant squealed and kicked and reached for the toy. He tapped her nose with it again. "The front's supposed to stay a while, too. It's good we came out today."

"She's flirting with you."

Royce looked back at Maggie, grinning. "She's going to be a real heart stealer someday."

"She's one already, I think," Maggie said softly. She pushed away from the table. "I better use the rest room before we leave. I'll be right back."

As Maggie left the table, the matron at the next stood also, preparing to leave. Royce glanced at her from the corners of his eyes. He'd become aware of her scrutiny after they first sat down, and several times during the course of their lunch he'd looked up to find the woman staring wistfully at them.

She dined alone, eating, he noted, with the quiet efficiency of one who did so often. Ancient yet ageless, she had fine, translucent skin like parchment. The jewels on her fingers spoke of wealth, as did her soft, cultured drawl. The waitress had seemed to know her, as had the manager who came over once during her meal. But both had related to her with the polite reserve one shows a customer rather than a friend.

The woman started past his table, then stopped.

"You have an adorable baby."

Royce glanced up, finding something about the woman's faded yet direct gaze unsettling. It was as if she could see right inside him. *What an active imagination he'd developed of late.*

He smiled at her. "Thank you."

"She looks like you."

He paused. "Most people think she looks like her mother."

The woman inclined her head. "In her coloring, certainly. But look at her bone structure, the shape of her face. She's the image of her daddy, as well."

Royce shifted his gaze to Amanda, feeling at once ridiculously proud and like a total fraud.

"You're a very lucky young man. You have a beautiful family." The woman clucked at Amanda, tickling her with a bony finger. She smiled, the wistfulness he'd seen earlier returning. "My Clarence and I weren't blessed with children, I'm afraid. It's too bad, he would have been a good daddy. Like you are."

She patted his arm. "Enjoy every moment, young man. Before you know it, everything will be changed."

Royce watched the woman walk away, her stride slow and pained with age. He swallowed past a lump in his throat, thinking of what she'd said.

Before you know it, everything will be changed.

And then you have nothing, Royce thought. And then you eat alone.

"I'm back." Maggie slipped into her seat. "We should probably go. It's already after one."

Royce turned and looked at her. She was smiling at him . . . only for him. She was so beautiful she seemed to glow. She made him glow.

He thought of Honoria then, and of her pending marriage. Brian would never make his sister feel this way. And this way was wonderful.

He swallowed and shifted his gaze to Amanda, who had begun to doze in her seat. Just looking at her made him feel ten feet tall and invincible.

You have a beautiful family. You're very lucky.

"Royce?"

He glanced back at Maggie. She was his wife. She loved him.

This was his family. He was lucky.

Even as he fought the feeling of jubilance that rose up in his chest, a tiny voice inside him told him to go with it. He'd only been as happy once in his life, he'd never laughed more.

He stood, unnerved to discover his hands shook. "You're right. We should go."

During the ride home, Maggie chatted, Amanda slept and his heart raced. As did his mind. He had a wonderful family; he was lucky. He would be a fool to let them slip away.

Go with it.

They arrived home and Maggie took Amanda up to put her down for her nap. Royce waited for her at the bottom of the stairs, pacing, fear and shock having given way to pure joy. He couldn't wait to tell Maggie she'd been right. He couldn't wait to pull her into his arms and ask her to be his wife again, to beg for the chance she had offered him ten days before.

"You're still here?"

Royce swung around. She stood at the top of the stairs, looking down at him, obviously perplexed. She wore blue jeans, a plain turtleneck sweater and cardigan. Nothing fancy or particularly provocative. Yet she stood there, a vision who made his world stand still and his heart race.

"Yes," he murmured. "I'm still here."

She started down. "I thought you would have run right off. You do know what time it is?"

"Yes." He worked to catch his breath. "I need to talk to you."

She frowned and searched his expression. "Is something wrong? You've hardly said two words since we left the restaurant."

She reached the bottom stair, and he tumbled her into his arms. She gasped as she landed against his chest.

"Royce, what—"

"I feel lucky, Maggie."

She tipped her head back, meeting his eyes. In hers he read a dawning realization and hope. "Lucky?" she repeated.

"Mmm, hmm." The phone rang; Royce tightened his arms around her. "Let the machine get it. What I have to say won't wait."

Maggie flattened her hands against his chest and laughed up at him. The phone sounded again. "It may be Honoria calling to fuss at you about being late."

"Tough."

"It may be Louise. She may have a problem at the coffeehouse."

"Let her solve it herself."

The phone jangled a last time; the machine picked it up. Royce caught her mouth in a breath-stealing kiss.

"Mrs. Adler," the woman's voice came over the machine's speaker, "this is Melanie Kane from Associated Charities. It's urgent that I speak with you and Mr. Adler. Something has come up and—"

Royce dropped his arms; Maggie ran to the phone. She picked it up just as Melanie began to hang up. "Hello," she said breathlessly. "Melanie?"

"Mrs. Adler?"

"Yes." Maggie curled her fingers around the phone cord. "What can I do for you?"

The woman paused. "I need to come by and talk to you and Mr. Adler."

Maggie glanced back at Royce. "Is something wrong?"

The woman paused again. "I'm on your side of the lake, can I come by now?"

"Now?" Maggie repeated, clutching the receiver. Royce crossed to where she stood, a question in his eyes. She looked at him helplessly.

"Mrs. Adler?"

"Yes . . . fine."

"Good. I'll be there in five minutes."

"Wait!" Maggie worked to control her runaway imagination. It was nothing, she assured herself. Just...nothing. She swallowed. "What's this about?"

"I'd rather talk to you both in person. I'll be right there."

Maggie replaced the receiver, her heart pounding. She turned and met Royce's eyes. "She knows. About us."

"Are you sure?" Royce drew his eyebrows together. "How could she have found out?"

Maggie brought a trembling hand to her mouth. "I don't know," she said, beginning to panic. "But she must. Oh, my God. What's going to happen? What if they—"

"Maggie." Royce caught her upper arms and lightly shook her. "Calm down. That doesn't make sense. How could she have found out?"

"I don't know." Maggie looked at him blankly. "But what else could it be? She sounded so serious, she sounded so...worried."

"It's probably just one of those surprise routine visits. If she sounded funny, it's probably because she's having a bad day."

"You really think so?"

"Sure." He put his arm around her shoulders. "We've got nothing to worry about."

But the moment they saw Melanie Kane's grim expression, they both knew that Royce had been wrong.

"Can I get you some coffee?" Maggie asked the woman nervously. "Some iced tea?"

"No, thank you." Melanie motioned toward the parlor. "Could we sit down?"

"Of course." Royce led her into the other room.

Once they were all seated, the woman glanced around, "Where's Amanda?"

Maggie gripped Royce's hand. "Napping."

"Good." The woman looked away, then back at them. She cleared her throat. "I have some news....It's not good, and I don't know quite where to begin to make this easier for you."

"Then just begin," Royce said brusquely, curling his fingers tighter around Maggie's.

"Amanda's birth mother wants to meet you."

Maggie stared blankly at the other woman. She shook her head. "Excuse me, but I must not have heard you correctly. You couldn't have said—"

"Amanda's birth mother wants to meet you."

Maggie's heart dipped crazily. She took a deep breath and searched the other woman's expression, looking for reassurance. It wasn't there. "This *is* just a routine thing. I mean, there's nothing for me...to...worry about?"

"I'm sorry." Melanie laced her fingers together. "She's having second thoughts."

Maggie brought a hand to her chest, fighting to catch her breath. "You can't be serious. After four and a half months...she's having second thoughts? There must be some mistake."

"There's no mistake. I'm so sorry." Melanie looked from one to the other. "But she hasn't said she wants

Amanda back. Right now, all she wants is to reassure herself that she made the right decision.''

Maggie fought back a wave of hysteria. This couldn't be happening. It was like every nightmare she'd ever had becoming a reality. What would she do if Amanda were taken away from her? How would she go on if she lost her?

"What kind of agency are you running?" Royce asked angrily. "I thought this was supposed to be a totally anonymous adoption."

"It was. But the birth mother has rights—"

"We have rights, too. What if we say no?"

Melanie clasped her hands in front of her. "That's your privilege, Mr. Adler. But the agency and I recommend you see her."

"Oh, God," Maggie said, light-headed, sucking in air. She looked up at Royce. "What are we going to do?"

"It's too early to panic," Melanie inserted quickly. "This is unusual but not unheard of."

"What about the surrender papers?" Royce demanded. "She signed them. We were granted the interlocutory decree."

"Nothing's carved in stone until the adoption's final. As you know, in this state that's six months from the time that decree is granted."

"This isn't right," he said, shaking his head. "It can't be right."

"I'm so sorry. I can't tell you how sorry..." The woman let her words trail off, looking helplessly first at Maggie, then Royce. "The law's specific here. There's nothing I can do."

"We'll get a lawyer."

"I'd suggest it, Mr. Adler." She stood. "But don't take too long. Right now she's anxious. She wants reassurance that she did the right thing. We may be able to keep this from escalating into a big deal. But if too much time passes, she's going to get—"

"A big deal?" Maggie repeated incredulously, following the woman to her feet. "She might want to take my baby away." She pressed a hand to her chest. "I feel like a part of me is dying, like my heart is being ripped from me." A sob caught in her throat. "I think that's a pretty damn big deal already. Now, you'll have to excuse me, because I can't . . ."

Turning, she fled from the room.

Royce let Melanie out, then went after Maggie. He found her in the nursery, just where he'd expected to find her. She stood beside the crib, her fingers wrapped around the top rail so tightly her knuckles were white. Her shoulders shook with silent sobs. He came up behind her, wanting so badly to comfort her he ached with the need.

But he didn't touch her, didn't speak. Instead he gazed at Amanda, a lump forming in his throat. She slept on her stomach. In the way of infants, she'd drawn her legs up under her; her right cheek rested on her folded hands so that her face was turned toward them. She was the picture of innocence, of beauty. Looking at her made him believe in miracles. He swallowed hard, the movement an effort.

"We could go away," Maggie said so softly at first he thought he'd misheard her. "We could go someplace where nobody knows us...someplace nobody would try to take her away."

"We can't do that, Maggie." He sucked in a sharp breath and touched her damp cheek. "You know we can't."

"But how can *she* have the right to do this?" Maggie turned and met his eyes, the anguish in hers ripping at him. "I've fed her and changed her and comforted her since she was six days old. I've walked her and rocked her for hours when she was fussy and nothing else would do. I sat up with her when she was sick. How can this woman come forward now and say she might...want..."

Tears choked her words, and she turned back to the crib. Reaching down, she gently stroked Manda's dark curls.

Royce put his hands on Maggie's shoulders and squeezed, unsure whether it was because he needed to comfort her or himself. "We'll get a lawyer," he murmured, working to keep his voice even, his tone calm. "We'll get the best adoption lawyer in the city. There have to be other options, Maggie. There have to be. It'll be okay. I swear it will."

Maggie looked over her shoulder at him, her eyes red and wet and so vulnerable they tore at him. She shook her head. "I want so badly to believe you. It hurts, I want so badly. But I...I've wanted like this before and—"

She caught her words, swallowing hard. "I'm so afraid. In my heart of hearts I know nothing will ever be all right again."

She turned her gaze back to Amanda. "She's my baby, Royce. I'm the only mother she's ever known. It's me she cries for... me she looks for. She doesn't know any other woman. How would she feel if one day I didn't come? What would she think? That I abandoned her? That I didn't love her? Oh, God... I can't bear it." She dropped her head into her hands, sobbing.

"Maggie..." Tears filled his own eyes, and he blinked against them. "Come here, sweetheart. It'll be all right." Royce eased her into his arms.

"No." She jerked away from him. "I'm not leaving her side. Not until I know everything's going to be okay."

Royce pushed away the hurt, the feeling of rejection and told himself to be an adult. Maggie was beside herself with grief; she needed his support, his calm. He held out a hand. "Maggie, you have to collect yourself. You have to try to think clearly."

"Collect myself?" she repeated angrily, whirling to face him. "How am I supposed to do that? I tell myself to be calm. I tell myself to be optimistic. But all I can feel is this hysteria, this fear so great it threatens to suffocate me. And all I can think is, what will I do if she's taken from me?"

Tears slid down her cheeks, and she shook her head. "You don't understand, Royce. You can't. Just go away. Just leave me alone."

"Maggie..."

She shook her head again, and he took a step back. His jubilation of earlier seemed ridiculously premature now, a cruel mockery. *Lucky?* He sucked in a deep breath. Right, he was lucky. For the space of minutes he'd realized that he had everything, and now he had...

He looked down at Amanda, his eyes burning with unshed tears. They couldn't lose her. He curled his hands into fists. No one would take her away. He wouldn't allow it to happen. There were always options. Always. He had to believe that.

He shifted his gaze back to Maggie, wanting to touch her, needing comfort so badly he shook. Her words of moments ago spun through his head, mixing with grief and hurt and desperation. She didn't want his advice or his comfort. She didn't want his arms.

He turned away from her and crossed to the door. He paused, but didn't look back. "I'm going into work. If you need anything, call." She didn't respond. "I'll get an appointment with an attorney. Is any time okay?"

"Yes."

"I'll see you tonight." Feeling colder than he had in months, he walked out of the nursery.

Although almost midnight by the time he returned home, lights burned throughout the house. Royce climbed the stairs, knowing he would find Maggie where he'd left her.

As expected, she was in the nursery, sitting in the rocking chair, Amanda asleep in her arms. She didn't look at him when he walked into the room.

"I tried to call. You didn't answer." She met his eyes. In hers, he saw exhaustion and grief. It was as if she'd given up already. "I found a lawyer. He'll see us tomorrow. He's the best, Maggie."

She nodded and leaned her head against the chair back. "What time?"

"Two." He rubbed his hands over his face and let out an exhausted breath. "Are you coming to bed?"

She shook her head. "No."

"Maggie . . . you can't stay here."

"I'm not going to leave her."

"Think of Amanda. She'll be more comfortable in her bed. She needs—"

"She needs her mother," Maggie said, tears choking her voice. "I'm her mother."

Royce opened his mouth, then closed it again. "Can I get you a blanket? A pillow?"

"I'm fine." Maggie looked down at Amanda and gently combed her fingers through the infant's hair. "Go on to bed. I don't need anything."

Royce stood there another moment, then jammed his hands into his pockets. "All right, Maggie. Good night."

As he stepped out into the hall, Alice's door opened and she peeked out. Her eyes were wide, her cheeks pale. She motioned to him, and he crossed to her.

"What's going on?" she whispered hoarsely. "Maggie was crying when I got home and . . . she wouldn't talk to me. She still won't." Alice drew in a trembling breath. "Have you done something to her? Because if you have, I'll..."

"I wish this were about me." Royce sighed and yanked at the knot of his tie. "It's not."

Alice shifted her gaze toward the nursery door, then looked back at him. "Then...what?"

Royce filled her in. As he did, her already colorless cheeks paled more. "You mean there's a chance Manda could be taken away?"

Royce nodded. "There's a chance. We've got an appointment with a lawyer tomorrow."

"Oh, no." Alice wrung her hands. "There must be something we can do..."

"I'm trying, Alice." He rubbed his hands wearily over his face. "Believe me, I'm doing everything I can."

"Poor Maggie."

Poor Maggie. That's Maggie's baby. Alice's words, his mother's, ran through his head. He didn't know why the words hurt so badly, but they did. He cleared his throat. "Look Alice, I'm dead on my feet. I've got to get some sleep."

"Sure." She straightened. "I'm okay."

He walked around her and without consciously deciding to, returned to the bedroom he'd first used upon moving back in with Maggie.

Chapter Twelve

The attorney's offices claimed the entire twenty-fourth floor of one of downtown New Orleans's newest and highest-priced pieces of real estate. He and Maggie had barely talked during the trip there, and their silence continued as they waited in the elegantly appointed reception area.

Royce watched Maggie as she tried to quiet Amanda. He'd done his best to convince her to leave the baby with Louise or Eileen, but she'd been adamant about bringing her. Now the infant refused to be calmed.

Royce frowned. "Why don't you let me hold her," he said, trying to smile. "Give your arms a break."

"No." Maggie shook her head, barely looking at him. "Thanks, but they don't need a break."

"But Manda does." Angry spots of color appeared on her cheeks, and he added, "Look at yourself, Maggie. You're totally distraught and you're clutching at her." He held out his arms. "She can't be comfortable."

Tears filled Maggie's eyes, and she blinked against them. "You're right," she whispered. "I'll relax. Just let me hold her."

Royce glanced away, the anguish in her eyes affecting him like a punch to his gut. He would give anything to make her hurt go away, but she'd withdrawn from him and wouldn't be comforted. All he could do was sit here and feel helpless.

And he hated the feeling.

"Mr. and Mrs. Adler?"

The man who approached them, hand outstretched, could be no other than their attorney. Royce stood and fitted his hand to the other man's. "James Wheeler, I presume."

"You presume correctly. It's a pleasure to meet you."

Wheeler was everything Royce had expected— power suit, brash good looks, a smile that was friendly but not quite warm. "Thanks for seeing us on such short notice."

"I hope I can help. Mrs. Adler." He turned to Maggie and nodded. "Beautiful child."

Maggie gazed down at Amanda, then looked back up at the man, her eyes glassy. "Thank you."

"Come this way."

He led them to his office. The large, richly furnished room attested to his position in the prestigious firm. After seating them at the conversation area on a wine-colored leather couch and offering them refreshment, he took a place on the couch that faced theirs. "Just to make sure I have everything, why don't you explain the facts of this situation to me again."

Royce recounted the story; the attorney jotted down an occasional note as he spoke. When he'd finished, the lawyer leaned thoughtfully back against the leather couch. "Mr. and Mrs. Adler—"

"Please, Royce and Maggie."

The man nodded. "Royce and Maggie, as far as the law's concerned you have two options here. You can agree to see this woman or you can refuse. Your caseworker was correct when she told you the laws concerning adoption are specific. The waiting period between the signing of the surrender papers, the interlocutory decree and the final adoption was designed specifically to protect both the adoptive and birth parents. It gives both parties a chance to reconsider before permanently and irrevocably accepting or signing away all rights to their child."

Royce heard Maggie's quickly indrawn breath and covered her hand with his. Although stiff and unresponsive beneath his, he curled his fingers around hers anyway. "To protect us?" he echoed incredulously, hoping the attorney wouldn't hear the tremor in his voice.

"I'm afraid, however, that until the adoption's final, the law weighs heavily on the side of the birth parents."

Maggie's fingers convulsed under his, and he tightened his grip. "So if the birth mother wants Amanda back, we just hand her over with a smile and a thanks for the opportunity to get totally attached to her baby?"

"Not at all." The man leaned forward, his expression earnest. "The birth mother can't show up at your door and demand the child back. She would have to hire a lawyer and take you to court. Of course, we would prepare the best case possible, in an attempt to convince the judge that the child should remain with you."

Without pausing he continued. "For instance, we would delve into her background to discover if she was or had ever been associated with any illicit or illegal activities. But even on the chance that we uncovered something of that nature, I have to warn you the court favors the biological parent—even in cases where the birth mother is unfit."

"What are you saying?" Royce asked, the words sticking in his throat. "That we would lose?"

"Most probably." The lawyer laced his fingers together. "There's a prevailing attitude in this country that children are the property of their birth parents rather than individuals with the same rights guaranteed you and me. Even in cases involving physical and mental abuse, neglect or involvement with illegal activities such as drugs or prostitution, judges remand children back into the custody of their biological parents again and again. Of course, this is more often the case with older children than infants, but it is indicative of the court's disposition."

Royce thought of Alice. Maggie had told him that the girl had been taken away from her parents several times, only to be sent back. How different her life could have been if a judge thought of her well-being instead of her parents' right to her.

Maggie looked at their beautiful Manda, then back at Wheeler. "That's sick."

"A lot of child-rights activists think so, too, and are working to change those laws. But for the time being we have to work within the system, the laws, we have." He tipped his hands palms-up. "I'm sorry."

"Doesn't the fact that I'm the only mother Amanda has known count for anything?" Maggie asked, her voice jagged with tears. "Doesn't it matter that she loves me?"

The attorney nodded. "That the child has bonded with you will be a big part of our case. We'll hire child psychologists to testify to the permanent harm that could be done to Amanda's ability to trust and love if separated from you. But—"

"Her lawyer will hire psychologists to refute ours' testimony," Royce supplied, frustrated.

"Yes. And she is, after all, not even six months old. If she were older, if she had lived with you for years, then that argument would carry more weight."

Amanda began to protest Maggie's grip on her, and Royce eased the infant from her arms. Maggie let her go but immediately curled her arms around her middle, hugging herself.

"I have already put my associates to work on finding cases that might serve as a precedent for ours, but frankly in the ones I found in which the judge awarded custody to the adoptive parents the facts were so far removed from those of our case that they just wouldn't be of any value to us. I'll keep looking, of course."

Royce bent his head to Amanda's and breathed in the sweet baby scent he'd come to know and love so well. His eyes filled with tears and, embarrassed, he fought them back, his throat and chest aching from the effort.

"You're telling us it's hopeless," Maggie whispered, lifting her eyes to the lawyer's, hers swimming with tears. "You're telling us we don't have a chance of . . . keeping her."

Royce saw the compassion in the attorney's eyes. And the frustration. But when he spoke his words were optimistic, his tone calm. "Not so fast, Maggie. Agree to see this woman. Try to nip this thing in the bud. As I understand it, she hasn't actually expressed the desire to take Amanda back."

He smiled sympathetically. "I know it's hard, but put yourself in her shoes. She gave birth to this baby— she wanted to do the right thing for her. Now she's frightened. She needs reassurance. She needs to see for herself that she has done the right thing. Give her what she needs. You're a good-looking couple. Amanda is healthy, obviously adored and thriving."

"In cases like this, does that usually work?" Maggie asked hopefully.

"Every case is different. It's going to depend on you two and the birth mother."

His pat answer was one hundred percent politician. But Royce saw the truth in his eyes: when the biological mother had second thoughts, it usually did not end happily for the adoptive parents.

"So that's it?" Royce lifted Amanda to his shoulder and stood. "There's nothing you can do for us."

"I'm sorry." Wheeler followed him to his feet. "I'll be happy to represent you, should this situation worsen. But I truly hope that's not necessary. There's every chance we're being premature here."

Neither Royce nor Maggie spoke as the attorney led them out of his office. There was nothing left to say; Wheeler had said it all. Royce rubbed Amanda's back as they walked to the elevator, murmuring soft words in her ear, unsure whether in an attempt to comfort her or himself.

They stepped into the empty elevator; the doors slid shut behind them. Still they didn't speak, and Royce angled a glance at Maggie. She looked much as she had in the attorney's office, arms wrapped around herself, her face pale, her expression bleak. His heart broke for her.

She met his gaze. "May I have my daughter back, please?"

Royce handed Manda back, and Maggie cuddled her. "Mommy loves you sweetie. Mommy's here.... She's right here."

Royce breathed deeply through his nose and tipped his face toward the ceiling, searching for calm, praying for the right words. There were no right words, he acknowledged. And calm...calm was for attorneys who made one hundred and fifty dollars an hour to deliver blows that didn't touch *them* at all.

He swallowed and turned his gaze once more to Maggie. "Wheeler was right. We can't jump the gun. Let's agree to see her, then move forward from there."

Maggie shook her head, but didn't look at him. "I don't want to talk."

Royce made a sound of frustration. "The time's come to talk, Maggie. Whether you want to or not. We have decisions to make, and neither one of us can make them alone."

"No." She pressed her lips against the top of Manda's head. "No."

Helplessness and anger welled inside him until he thought he might burst. He slammed his fist against the emergency stop button, the car shuddered to a halt and the alarm sounded. He wheeled around and faced her. "We're going to talk, Maggie. Now."

"What do you want to talk about?" she demanded, her tone edged with hysteria. "I heard everything that man said. He told us it's practically hopeless. He told us our only chance is a long shot."

"Maggie..."

He reached out to touch her; she slapped his hands away. "Do you want me to say that I can live without her? That everything will be okay? I can't say those words.... I don't believe they're true."

She tried to turn from him; he caught her elbow and forced her to look him in the eye. "Dammit, Maggie.... Don't shut me out."

She flung her head back. "Aren't you the one who said those doors had been closed and locked a long time ago?"

"Things have changed since then. At least I thought they had." Amanda began to whimper, and he lowered his voice. "Let me help you, Maggie. Let's comfort each other." He put his hands on her shoulders. "We'll face this together. Whatever the outcome, we'll—"

She jerked away from his touch. "Face this together?" she repeated bitterly. "Go on, no matter the outcome? Does the outcome even matter to you? You never wanted Amanda.... You never wanted children, at all. What do you want now, Royce? What do you feel? Relief?"

He recoiled from her, her words slamming into him, stunning him. Everything he'd told himself since this had happened—that she needed time, that she hurt—had been justification only, a way to ignore the real truth.

Amanda was all she'd ever wanted.

She'd made that abundantly clear. He just hadn't wanted to see.

Furious, aching, he threw the switch and the elevator started up again. He'd been a fool. He'd actually believed there was a chance for them, had believed her when she said she loved him without strings.

A fool. He'd been such a fool.

If only it didn't hurt so damn bad. If only he'd protected himself. After their separation he'd promised himself he would never allow himself to be devastated like that again. Now he hurt more. Because for one brief and golden moment he'd thought he had it all.

You have a beautiful family. You're a lucky young man.

The matron's words rang in his head, mocking him. But if those words had been a mockery, her next had been a prophecy. *Before you know it, everything will be changed.*

The elevator stopped; the doors slid open. He and Maggie alighted from the car and crossed the foyer to the building's mammoth front doors. The cold front had arrived and the wind tore at him as they exited the building. He welcomed the wind's sting because it was real.

As Maggie's love had never been.

He'd parked a block away from the building. They walked quickly, Maggie cuddling Amanda to her in an attempt to shield her from the cold. But the infant began to cry anyway. She wouldn't be consoled and cried the whole way home, the sound of her distress a fitting accompaniment to their silence.

Royce pulled into their driveway but didn't turn off the car's engine. No matter what the outcome with Amanda, he and Maggie were finished. As soon as the adoption was settled, he would start divorce proceedings.

He tightened his fingers on the steering wheel, fighting off the cold, the feeling of betrayal. "Are we agreed on meeting with the birth mother?" he asked, keeping his eyes straight ahead.

"We have no other choice."

"Shall I call Melanie and arrange the time and place?"

"Please." Maggie climbed out of the car. As she started to close the door, she paused. "Royce?"

He turned his face to hers, then wished he hadn't. In her eyes he thought he saw something soft and brimming with regret, something akin to a plea. He called himself an idiot. "Royce, I—"

He cut her off. "Amanda's cold. You better go in."

Maggie gazed at him for a moment, then nodded and stepped away from the car. Without another word, she shut the door and walked away.

Royce made the call, and between him, Melanie and the birth mother, they decided the meeting would take place the following afternoon at his and Maggie's house in Mandeville.

Melanie had been relieved by their decision and had tried to reassure him. He told her to call Maggie.

Royce stared blankly at the press proofs of Sassy's new menus and wondered if Melanie had called Maggie. Maggie hadn't mentioned it, but then he and Maggie didn't talk anymore.

He picked up one of the proofs, then tossed it back onto his desk. The advertising agency had dropped them by first thing that morning and wanted them back as soon as possible. The printer was waiting for his okay to start the presses back up.

Royce checked his watch for about the fiftieth time since climbing out of bed. Two hours. Only two more hours until he and Maggie faced the woman whose intentions had haunted their last days and nights. In two hours the suspense would be over.

Royce sucked in a deep breath. The minute he saw the woman, he would know what her intentions were.

He would know then and there if she meant to break their hearts.

But the wait was agony.

As would be living without Maggie.

He pressed the heels of his hands to his eyes. He'd been a fool to think he would get anything done today; his head—and heart—was home with Manda and Maggie.

Royce dropped his hands and tipped his face toward the ceiling. He loved Amanda; he *was* her father. He would do anything, give anything, to protect her from harm. He would sacrifice for her happiness . . . and the sacrifice would be a joy. He shook his head at the irony—it had taken the threat of losing her to make him see the truth. But he saw now.

And the truth terrified him. He loved her and couldn't bear the thought of losing her.

How had it happened? How had he gone from feeling nothing to feeling everything? Dear Lord, how had the man who professed not to believe in love, the man who feared he had no love to give, become one who loved so much he ached, one who had so much to give he thought he might burst with it?

He tightened his jaw in determination. If the adoption did go through, he would be Amanda's legal father. And no matter what occurred between him and Maggie, he would take his rightful place in her life.

Maggie.

They had hardly spoken in the aftermath of their meeting with Wheeler, and the words they had exchanged could hardly have been called a conversation. They existed as strangers under the same roof, the situation a painful recreation of the past.

He missed her. Everything about her. He missed the way she made him feel.

He missed his family.

The phone rang and he jumped, automatically picking it up. "Royce Adler," he answered absently, wishing he'd let someone out front get it.

"Mr. Adler, this is Officer Gill from the NOPD juvenile division."

Royce straightened, his attention fully on the caller now. Donations, he told himself. Time for the police ball or the circus for handicapped kids. "What can I do for you, Officer Gill?"

"I hate to bother you, but we have an Alice Dougherty down here. She says you're her guardian."

Royce went blank for a moment, then his heart began to hammer against the wall of his chest. *Alice had been arrested. Alice was in trouble.*

"That's right, officer," Royce said quietly, his chest tight. "Is there a problem?"

The officer explained that she had been caught shoplifting and that the store was pressing charges. When he finished, Royce let out a silent, relieved breath. It could have been worse, he told himself. It could have been drugs; she could have been hurt.

He tightened his fingers on the receiver. Thank God she hadn't been hurt.

After getting the officer to tell him where she'd been caught and exactly what she'd taken, he promised he would come right down.

He hung up the phone, then picked it back up, dialing the number of the store in question, the Uptown Boutique. Over the years the Adlers had been very good customers.

Five minutes and many pulled strings later, he'd gotten the owner to agree to not press charges.

He shrugged into his jacket, snatched up the press proofs and checked his watch. He should have just enough time to take care of Alice and get back to Mandeville for his and Maggie's meeting with Amanda's birth mother.

"Honoria—" he burst into his sister's office "—I've got to go. You'll have to proof these." He tossed the menus on her desk. "The agency wants them back ASAP."

She raised her eyebrows. "Sorry, little brother. This is your department and my plate's full today."

"I've got an emergency. I won't be back."

"Wait a minute!" He ignored her and started out the door. She flew to her feet. "We have two private parties tonight and a full reservation book."

"And we have a staff of highly skilled people for just such occasions." He cleared his throat and checked his watch. "Look, Honoria, I'm sorry to dump this on you, but it's Alice. I've got to go."

She snatched up her cigarettes and lighter. "Royce, a minute. Please. There's something ... I have to say to you."

The tremor in her voice made him stop. He looked at her, seeing for the first time that she was troubled. He lifted his eyebrows in question.

"I was across the lake yesterday and stopped by your house. I needed to—" She shook her head and drew in a deep, shaky breath. "I talked to Maggie and...she told me what's going on."

She met his eyes again; he saw that hers were glassy. "Amanda's beautiful, Royce. I can only imagine what you're feeling. And I only wish—" Again she shook her head, fighting to gain control of her emotions. "If there's anything I can do, any way I can help...please don't hesitate to ask."

Royce blinked, feeling ridiculously young and closer to his sister than he ever had. "That means...everything to me, Honoria. I'll call you later."

"Royce?"

He stopped at the door once more.

"You'll tell Maggie I'm thinking of her?"

"I'll tell her."

He made it from Honoria's office to the police station's juvenile division in record time. To do so, he broke more laws than he cared to think of, especially considering the circumstances.

He found Alice slumped in a chair, pale and shaking and trying valiantly to act cocky when it was obvious all she wanted to do was cry. Torn between concern and anger at the stupidity of her actions, he made the necessary arrangements to get her released.

When he signed the last form, he turned and faced her. "You've got some explaining to do, young lady."

She opened her mouth, and he cut her off. "When we get out of here." He caught her elbow and steered her toward the stairs. "Until then, you'd better be thinking of a damn good reason for having done this."

She followed him to the car, head down, shoulders slumped. He unlocked the sedan's passenger door, then went around to the other side and slid behind the wheel. He shut the door and silence stretched between them.

Royce looked at her from the corners of his eyes. He hadn't the faintest idea what to say, he realized. Nor the first clue to which words would be the right ones.

He did know, though, that bellowing at her would be a mistake, so he breathed deeply through his nose and counted to ten. Then fifteen. He turned to her. "Well, Alice?"

She folded her arms across her chest and jutted out her chin. "Well, what?"

Now she developed an attitude. He curled his fingers around the steering wheel. "How long has this behavior been going on?"

She looked at him defiantly. "That figures. You probably think I'm a kleptomaniac or something."

He tightened his fingers. "I could let the facts speak for themselves, but I'm not doing that. I don't have time to play games with you, Alice. Was this the first time you've done something like this, or not?"

Her shoulders slumped again. "The first time."

He stared at her, believing her despite all logic which told him to do otherwise. "Why did you do it, Alice? Why today?"

"I don't know." She hung her head. "I just didn't think."

"I'll say." Royce let out a pent-up breath. "Don't you realize the kind of pressure Maggie's under? Don't you care about her at all?"

Alice jerked her head up and met his eyes, her expression one of pure anguish. As she gazed at him, her eyes filled and her lips began to tremble.

"Oh, Alice, don't do tha—"

She burst into tears.

Her shoulders shook with her great, gasping sobs; Royce swallowed and gathered her awkwardly into his arms. He patted her back. "It's okay," he murmured. "It's all right. Let's calm down and talk about this."

She nodded, her breath catching as she tried to stop her tears. It took several moments, but her sobs finally subsided into hiccups.

She pulled away, wiping her eyes self-consciously. He handed her a handkerchief, and she blew her nose. "I do care about Maggie," she stammered. "More than . . . anything."

She looked back up at him, her eyes swimming still with tears. "Please don't tell her about this. Please. I won't do it ever again. I promise."

The tears threatened once more, and Royce saw how she fought to check them. He admired much about Alice, her courage and pride, the fact that she'd endured so much and still had a softness and an ability to love. Shoplifting wasn't her style, nor were lying and sneaking around. Alice had too much good in her, too much hope.

"Why did you do it?" he asked softly. "You had to know it would hurt Maggie. You had to know she wouldn't be able to handle it, not today."

Alice wrung her hands. "I don't know why I did it."

Playing the hunch he'd had all those weeks ago when he and Maggie had caught her sneaking into the house, Royce put his hand under her chin and tipped her face up to his. "This is about Maggie, isn't it? And Amanda?"

Alice stared at him, her tears spilling silently over. She nodded. His heart ached for her, but he pressed anyway. "You're jealous of Amanda. You wish Maggie had never gotten her."

"No!" She shook her head. "I mean, I don't dislike her. I never wanted Maggie to lose her. It's just that I ... know ... she ..."

Tears choked her words, and Royce covered her hand with his. "It's just what, Alice? You think Maggie doesn't need you anymore?"

She nodded again and hugged herself. "But I don't blame her for wanting Amanda ... She's so cute and sweet. I know I can't compete with her."

Royce curled his fingers around Alice's, her words striking chords deep inside himself. Her behavior today and all those weeks ago had been about needing attention, needing to feel important and loved. And about fear.

"You don't have to compete, Alice," he said softly. "Maggie still needs you."

"No." She inched her chin up bravely even though defeat clouded her eyes. "I wasn't her first choice. She took me in only because she needed to give back. You know, help somebody like she was helped. That's cool, but...it's not love. I don't really matter to her."

"Oh, Alice..." Royce gathered her into his arms once again. She resisted, but still he held her. That he wanted so badly to help her terrified him—but warmed him more.

"Maggie's going through a hard time right now," he murmured, stroking Alice's hair. "We both are. But believe me, she still needs you. Now more than ever. She loves you, Alice. Amanda can't take your place. Nobody can."

Alice shook her head, her breath coming in short gasps as she fought back tears. "Why would she want me when she has Amanda... When she has you?"

"Maggie has enough love for us all. Love isn't exclusive. Just because she loves Amanda doesn't mean she can't love you. And love doesn't have a pecking order, it's all equal and all wonderful."

As he said the words, he realized he believed them, really believed them. Astonished, he pulled back so he could see Alice's eyes. As if the sun had broken over the horizon for the very first time, he felt warmed, bathed in light. And as if a giant weight had been lifted from his shoulders, he felt as if he could soar with eagles.

All along, since Maggie had first broached the subject of children, then later when she'd proposed that Alice live with them, he'd been afraid of losing her, of her not loving him anymore. Just as Alice feared Maggie no longer loved or needed her now.

His fears had been unfounded, born out of a childhood bereft of affection. Out of a lifetime of yearning for love. He'd been wrong about so many things.

He grinned at Alice, then laughed out loud. He'd never stopped loving Maggie. Out of fear and a need to protect himself, he'd denied his love for her.

Royce smiled at Alice, seeing her confusion. He must appear either a madman or an idiot right now. He laughed at the image, kissed her forehead and released her.

"You and I are a lot alike, Alice. I pushed Maggie away because I thought she couldn't love me and a child. But I see now that when love's shared it grows stronger. It's doubled and tripled. She has plenty of love for all of us." He laughed again. "And so do I."

Alice twisted her fingers together and searched his expression. "I want to believe you. I want it to be true more than anything."

"I know," he murmured, squeezing her fingers. "Trust someone who's been there on this. It is true."

"What about Amanda?" Alice asked. "What's going to happen to her?"

Amanda. He checked his watch and swore. They had just enough time to get across the causeway and home to meet the birth mother as she walked through the door. If they flew.

"It's going to be all right, Alice. Somehow, even if I have to get down on my knees and beg, it's going to be all right." He started the car. "Buckle your safety belt, kiddo. This plane's about to take off."

Chapter Thirteen

Amanda dozed in her playpen, set up in the warmest spot in the kitchen. Maggie gazed at her, smiling tenderly. For the meeting with her biological mother, she'd dressed Amanda in a bright red fleecy romper with multicolored bows down the front. She tied a red ribbon in her dark curls; her fuzzy socks had red pompoms attached to the front. She looked adorable.

Maggie's smile faded. Melanie had stressed that the birth mother would want to see Amanda. She'd warned, too, that the woman—Sarah was her name—would probably want to hold her and had advised them to do whatever necessary to reassure her.

Maggie curled her fingers into her palms. But who would reassure them?

The taste of fear in her mouth, Maggie took one last look at Amanda, then checked the clock for what seemed like the billionth time since she'd climbed out of bed that morning.

Twenty more minutes.

Where was Royce?

He'll be here, she told herself, swallowing hard. Any moment he'll race through the door. Maggie clasped her hands together and glanced almost frantically around the already immaculate kitchen. She needed something to do, something to occupy her hands and her brain. She'd already made coffee. And iced tea. She had a plate of her best chocolate chip cookies, baked fresh an hour ago, out and waiting.

Cookies. A hysterical laugh bubbled to her lips. Did one offer refreshments in a situation such as this? Did one pretend this meeting was no more than a social call, pretend the outcome of it couldn't change her life forever?

Stay calm, she told herself. Her palms were damp and she rubbed them together. The birth mother would not be reassured by a basket case.

A basket case.

That was what she had been since the afternoon three days before when Melanie Kane had called, and as often as she told herself to get a grip on her emotions, the truth was she'd fallen apart.

Maggie shifted her gaze to her sleeping daughter, then back to the clock. Fifteen minutes.

Where was he?

Maggie went to the window above the door, pushed aside the sheer and looked out at the brilliant day. And the empty drive. She caught her bottom lip between her teeth. Royce wouldn't abandon her. Not now when she needed him most. Not ever.

As the truth of that filtered through the fog of fear that had encompassed her since Melanie Kane's phone call, she brought a trembling hand to her mouth. Dear Lord, what had she done?

She turned away from the window and leaned her back against the door. Through this whole thing Royce had been committed to her, caring and supportive. He'd tried to ease her pain, had tried to lift her spirits. Again and again he had reached out to her.

In return, how had she treated him?

Tears sprang to her eyes as she thought of the things she'd said to him, of the way she'd jerked away from his touch and slapped at his hands when he'd tried to comfort her.

She covered her face with her hands. She'd accused him of being relieved that they might lose Manda. How could she have been so insensitive, so cruel?

He loved Amanda. She was his baby, too.

Maggie pushed away from the door and on trembling legs, crossed to the big oak table in the center of the room and sank onto one of the chairs set around it. His feelings had been plain to see—they'd been in his eyes and voice at the lawyer's, in the way he'd held on to Amanda as if terrified to lose her, in the way he played with her, watched her, talked to her.

He'd been as devastated by this as she.

Maggie dropped her head into her hands. His feelings *should* have been plain to see, but she'd been too wrapped up in her own fear and grief to see even the obvious. Let alone help him.

Just as she had at five years old when she realized her mother wasn't coming back, she'd jailed herself alone with her grief.

In the process, she'd hurt him. Badly.

She lifted her eyes once more to the clock. Ten minutes. Dear Lord, what if something had happened to him? What would she do?

No. She closed her hands into fists. No more "what ifs." She wasn't a child anymore. Today she stopped waiting for her world to fall apart, stopped expecting to end up alone and hurting.

Maggie shook her head. All along she'd thought she had let her marriage, her love, slip away. The truth was, she'd thrown them away. Twice now. Weeks ago, she had asked Royce for another chance. But she hadn't really believed in that chance. She had expected to lose Royce. Just as she had expected to lose Manda.

The time had come to stop allowing the fears of a child to interfere in the life of an adult. The little girl whose mother had abused and abandoned her had grown into a woman. A strong woman, one deserving of happiness and love.

Maggie stood, straightened her shoulders and lifted her chin. She hadn't lost Royce. She loved him; she *was* the right woman for him. And she didn't care who thought otherwise. Starting now, this moment, she began making up to him—and herself—for the way she'd hurt them both.

Amanda cooed in her sleep and Maggie crossed to the playpen. She squatted down beside it and gazed at her beautiful daughter, love welling in her chest.

She *was* Amanda's mother.

Somehow she would prove it to the woman who had given birth to her.

Hearing tires on the shell drive, she turned and raced to the door, her heart in her throat. *Please let it be Royce. Please let him be okay.*

It was Royce. He climbed out of the car, the breeze ruffling his fair hair and lifting his tie, the sun glinting off his sunglasses. He looked up as she flung the door open.

He was here; he was all right. Thank God.

She ran down the steps to the drive. He held out his hands; she grasped them. She met his eyes and saw his hesitation, his surprise. She squeezed his fingers, wanting to tell him now, everything she had realized, everything she felt.

But now wasn't the time. Now they had another mountain to scale. She would tell him everything later.

"It's going to be all right," she whispered. "We're not going to lose Manda."

"No."

Emotion choked even that one word, and Maggie's heart wrenched. She'd been so unfair. If it took the rest of her life, she would make it up to him.

Maggie turned her gaze to Alice's then, wondering for the first time why she had arrived with Royce. At the teenager's pale face and puffy eyes, she drew her eyebrows together in concern. "Are you all right, Alice?"

Alice looked at Royce in a way Maggie could only describe as pleading, then down at her feet. "I'm fine." She stuffed her hands into the pockets of her denim jacket. "I could...hang around. I mean, if you want me to."

Maggie realized at that moment both how grateful she was for Alice and how badly she had treated her these past few days. Regret washed over her. In her fear, she had hurt the people she loved most.

"That would be a big help, Alice." She reached over and clasped her hand. "I don't know what to...expect from this meeting. It'll be comforting to know you're here." She squeezed the girl's fingers, then released them. "I appreciate your support more than you know."

Alice looked away, her eyes suspiciously bright. "No problem."

"We better go in," Royce said softly. "She'll be arriving any moment."

Royce had been right. No sooner had they closed the door behind them and Alice had headed upstairs, than they heard a car in the drive. Maggie's heart flew to her throat, her bravado of earlier not quite able to stand up to reality. She pushed the "what ifs" out of her mind, but her terror would not be quelled. It, like her love for Amanda, knew no bounds.

"Maggie."

She met Royce's eyes.

"I'm here for you."

Those words comforted her to an extent she hadn't thought possible right now. She laced her fingers with his and held tight. "I don't know what I'd do without you."

"You'll never have to find out." He brought her hand to his lips, then released it. "Ready?"

"As much as I'll ever be." Sucking in a deep breath she went to the door, opening it a moment before the woman knocked.

Amanda's birth mother wasn't what she'd expected. Pretty, with a medium build and large, light eyes. Her hair was fair instead of dark, straight instead of curly. Nor was she the teenager Maggie had imagined she would be. She appeared to be in her mid-twenties.

Amanda had gotten her eyes.

The realization shook her. Recognizing a physical connection between her daughter and her biological mother somehow made the woman more real, more a part of Amanda.

She didn't want her to be real, Maggie acknowledged. She didn't want to admit that any other woman had a claim on her Manda—not an emotional one, not even a genetic one.

But she couldn't change the truth. Even if it cut clean to her soul.

Maggie told herself to speak, to move away from the door and invite the woman in, but she couldn't bring herself to do more than stare at her. She and this woman were total strangers, yet in one very special way, totally connected. This stranger had given her the most wonderful gift in the world, yet she could take it away again.

Goose bumps raced up her arms as conflicting emotions tumbled through her—love and fear, hope and desperation. She wanted to hug the woman, she wanted to beg her not to take Amanda away, she wanted to grab Manda and run as fast and far as she could.

The woman, Sarah, stared back at her, obviously as unnerved, as terrified as she. Maggie found that common ground, that shared fear, somehow comforting.

She tried to smile. "Sarah?"

The woman nodded and wiped her palms against her thighs. "Maggie?"

She nodded and swung the door wider. Her legs trembling, she stepped aside. "Come in."

Sarah entered the kitchen; Maggie closed the door behind her. "This is my husband, Royce."

Royce shook her hand. "How do you do?"

"Fine. Thanks." She rubbed her palms on her thighs again. "You have a lovely home."

"Thank you." Maggie folded her arms across her chest, then dropped them back at her sides. "Would you like some coffee or iced tea?"

"No." Sarah shook her head. "I don't want you to go to any trouble."

"It's no trouble. Both are already made." Maggie took some cups and saucers from the cabinets, hearing the edge of desperation in her voice and trying to quiet it. "I made cookies, too."

"All right, then. Coffee. Light and sweet."

Maggie poured her a cup, her hands shaking so badly she sloshed some onto the counter. "Royce?"

"Coffee." He smiled, trying to reassure. "Thanks."

Maggie placed the cups and the cookies on the table. "Please, sit down."

Sarah didn't move, and Maggie followed her gaze. She'd spotted the playpen and was staring at it, naked yearning in her eyes. Maggie began to shake.

"Did you know I'm a baker?" she asked quickly, stepping between her and her view of the playpen. "That's how Royce and I met. I brought him a piece of cake to try. For his restaurant, I mean." She laughed nervously. "This cookie recipe is one of my best. Here—" she held the plate out to her "—try one."

"Thanks, but...no." Sarah shook her head, her gaze still riveted on that corner of the kitchen. "Really, I couldn't eat a thing."

Maggie looked helplessly at Royce; he returned her gaze. In his she saw the same helplessness, the same frustration.

Amanda awakened then and began to softly cry. Maggie hurried to the playpen and scooped her up, cuddling her protectively against her chest. She didn't want to turn around. She didn't want Sarah to see Amanda.

If she did, how could she not want her back?

She squeezed her eyes shut. Please let it be okay, she prayed. Please give me the courage to get through this.

Taking a deep, steadying breath, she turned and crossed back to Royce's side.

"You named her Amanda?" Sarah asked thickly.

"Yes," Maggie managed. Royce laid a hand on her arm and she drew a deep breath, comforted by his support. "We call her Manda."

"Manda," the woman repeated softly, reaching out to touch her, then dropping her hand. "That's pretty."

"Her... daddy came up with it."

This time when Sarah reached out, she didn't drop her hand. Maggie tried not to cringe as she stroked Amanda's cheek.

"May I hold her?"

Maggie stared at the other woman, her world going black with fear. She'd been warned this might happen. But warnings were a far cry from reality. Placing Amanda back into her birth mother's arms was the realization of every nightmare she'd had since the moment Amanda had come into her life.

Maggie tightened her grip on Amanda, a dozen reasons why she couldn't allow Sarah to hold her jumping to her tongue.

"Please," she whispered. "I just want to hold her."

Royce stepped in. "Of course you can, Sarah."

He gently pried the infant away from her. Maggie bit her lip to keep from crying out as he placed Amanda in the other woman's arms.

Sarah bent her head to Amanda's and brushed her lips across her cheek. "She's so soft," she murmured. "And so pretty."

Maggie brought her fist to her mouth. The woman wanted Amanda back. They had lost her. Blinking against the tears welling in her eyes, she looked away. Her gaze landed on the three cups of cooling coffee and the plate of cookies, all still untouched.

It took everything she had not to whimper. As if knowing that, Royce put his arm around her. She lifted her eyes to his, even in her grief wanting him to know what he meant to her. He was her rock and her support. He was her love, her husband.

Royce met her gaze, his, too, moist and filled with love. And pain.

"I had to see her," Sarah said suddenly, her voice rough with tears. "I had to know she was okay. I had to know she was loved." She stroked Amanda's curls. "I wanted to make sure she was safe."

The tenderness in her eyes as she gazed down at Amanda made Maggie's knees weak. She held on to Royce and prayed.

"I thought about raising her on my own. For the first few months I was pregnant I even convinced myself that I could do it. Even though I was alone and could hardly support myself, even though it would be tough."

She looked at Maggie, then Royce. "But I realized she deserved more. I wanted her to have more. The advantage of both a mother and father. A real family."

The woman smiled down at Amanda, laughing a little as the baby gurgled back up at her. "That you had money wasn't important to me. I wanted to make sure you had love. Do you understand what I mean?"

Without waiting for an answer, she sank onto one of the kitchen chairs and continued. "My parents' marriage was one bloody battle after another that finally and mercifully ended in divorce. That doesn't matter," she went on, her eyes filling with tears, "except that I wanted so much more for...Amanda."

Her tears spilled over and she brushed at them with her free hand. "And then, after I'd given her up, I started thinking. And worrying. I had to see you for myself. Together. I had to be certain you had the kind of marriage that would enrich her life.''

Maggie stared at the woman, realizing for the first time, and with a thunderbolt, what she had done. Before today, this moment, she'd thought her lie of all those months ago hurt no one. She'd known she would be a good mother. She'd never doubted her capacity to love Amanda or provide a good home for her.

But she'd thought only in terms of fooling the adoption agency. Amanda's birth mother had been a shadowy image, a word only, certainly not a flesh-and-blood human being. Not a person who had fears and hopes and love for the life she had carried in her womb—the life, the child, Maggie now considered hers with every fiber of her being.

A sob caught in her throat and she clutched Royce's hand. She'd done the worst kind of disservice to this brave and loving young woman. This woman who had wanted nothing more than the best for the child she'd known she couldn't keep and care for.

She gazed at Sarah, tears pooling in her eyes and brimming over. What could she say to her now? How could she beg her forgiveness, atone for this sin?

And when she told her the truth, would they have a hope of keeping Amanda.

"I never knew," Royce said suddenly, quietly, "that a child could be so wonderful. I never knew I could love so much or so completely."

He met Maggie's eyes, love shining unabashedly from them. "Once upon a time there was a man who thought he had no love to give, a man who thought love to be somewhere and something just beyond his reach. Then along came a woman, a wonderful, beautiful woman. A woman with warmth and laughter. And love. So much love that the man felt alive for the very first time in his life.''

He caught Maggie's hand and laced his fingers with hers. ''He married the woman, and theirs was a union of love. Although, as with many married people, sometimes they didn't recognize how much they had. Or how lucky they were.''

He gazed at Maggie a moment more, then shifted his eyes back to Sarah. ''They were happy, yet the woman wanted a child more than anything. But she could never conceive.''

He crossed to where Sarah sat with Amanda and squatted down in front of her. ''Then into their lives came a miracle. Another life. A child so perfect, so full of beauty and love. And their happiness was complete.''

He reached out to Amanda, she grasped his finger and gurgled. ''These two are the man's world—his miracles.'' He looked into Sarah's eyes. ''I couldn't imagine life without them.''

Maggie came up behind Royce. She put her hands on his shoulders, moved beyond words by his love, loving him so much in return she wondered how her heart could hold it all.

To love Amanda they'd had to completely open their hearts. To keep her they would have to do the same. She took a deep, healing breath. ''I've been a wreck since Melanie called us about you,'' she began softly. "I was so afraid...you would take Amanda away from us. I still am."

She tightened her fingers on Royce's shoulders. "You see...I love her so much, I don't know how I would go on if I lost her. Maybe that sounds neurotic. Maybe it is. But I only know what I feel."

At the sound of her mother's voice, Amanda cooed and kicked in recognition. Maggie reached around Royce and caressed her cheek. "I bonded with Amanda the moment I laid eyes on her. And from the first moment I was her mother. In every way. It didn't matter that she didn't come from my body, because she was of my heart."

Maggie sucked in another deep breath, using the moment to collect herself, calm herself. "The terrifying thing about loving so much, so completely, is the bit of fear you keep locked up inside, the fear that comes out every once in a while as an almost paralyzing 'what if.' Love is laying your soul bare, chancing unbelievable joy...and total devastation."

Taking a deep breath, she continued. "You came into our lives. The most frightening 'what if' of all for me and Royce. For any adoptive parent. I hadn't thought about you...I hadn't been able to. You see, I didn't want to share Amanda. I didn't want to face the fact that some other woman might have claim on my daughter. I tell you this so you'll know the depth of my love for Amanda and understand my fear of you."

Maggie looked down at Royce. He tipped his head back and met her eyes. "As with Amanda, it seems like I've loved Royce forever. We've had our rough times, there isn't a couple that hasn't. But I'm completely devoted to him. I couldn't imagine my life without him. And I would fight to keep him and my marriage safe."

He reached up and caressed her cheek; she caught his fingers and brought them to her mouth. "This is my family." She looked pleadingly at the other woman. "Please...please don't take Manda away from us."

Silence stretched between them, taut with emotion. Sarah's eyes were wet, as were her own and Royce's. Maggie wished there was more she could say, wished she had magic on the tip of her tongue. But she'd used all her magic—the stuff of her heart. She could only pray it would be enough.

Amanda began to fuss, squirming and straining in Sarah's arms. The woman gazed down at her, tears sliding down her cheeks, splashing onto the infant's. She wiped the moisture gently away, then pressed a kiss to the top of Amanda's head.

She looked back up at Maggie. "I think she wants her mother," she whispered.

A cry of relief and joy bubbled to Maggie's lips and she held out her arms. Sarah placed Amanda in them and Maggie hugged her daughter to her chest.

"Is there anything I can do for you, Sarah?" Royce asked quietly. "If you need anything, if you ever—"

"Thank you," she whispered, cutting him off. "But I'm doing okay." She dug in her purse for a tissue and pressed it to her eyes. "Better than in a long time."

She stood and started for the door, then stopped and turned back to them. "I want you to know that I do understand, Maggie. And that I'll think about her.

But I'll never worry. And I'll never be sorry. Thank you so much for loving her.''

With Amanda still in her arms, Maggie closed the distance between them and hugged the other woman. "No, Sarah. Thank you. We could never repay you for the gift you've given us. When Amanda's old enough, we'll tell her about you. We'll tell her how wonderful and brave you were. We'll tell her you loved her.''

Royce joined them, standing behind Maggie, his hands on her shoulders. For long moments they clung to each other, then Sarah pulled away. She wiped her eyes, whispered goodbye and without looking back walked away.

Chapter Fourteen

Arms around each other, Amanda cuddled between them, Maggie and Royce watched Sarah walk away. When her car had disappeared from sight, Maggie turned and pressed her face into the crook between his neck and shoulder and breathed in the scent of him. Her husband. Her love.

She tipped her head back to meet his eyes. His were damp with emotion. She smiled tenderly. It seemed impossible that not so long ago her sister Louise had called him, this man who felt so deeply, an iceberg, and she'd not found the words to defend him.

She laid her open hand over his heart. It beat strong and steady beneath her palm. Comforting. Renewing. "There's so much I want to tell you," she whispered. "So much I want to share."

"And I you," he murmured, combing his fingers through her hair. "But we have forever to talk to each other. Right now there's someone who needs to hear our good news."

Alice. His first thought had been for the person they'd fought so bitterly over only a year ago. He'd changed much, this man she loved. And so, thank goodness, had she. She smiled. "You'll watch Manda?"

"You don't even have to ask." Grinning, he lifted Amanda high in the air. She squealed and kicked with delight.

Tears brimmed again. Maggie stood on tiptoes and pressed her mouth to his. "I love you, Royce Adler. Wait for me."

"Forever."

There was that word again. *Forever.* She replayed it in her head, reveling in the sound. She would never get enough of hearing it. Smiling brilliantly, she blew him a kiss. "I promise it won't take nearly that long."

She left the kitchen and started upstairs to the sound of her husband laughing with their daughter.

Maggie tapped on Alice's bedroom door, then peeked inside. Alice was curled up at the head of her bed, headphones on, a pillow bunched up on her lap. Late-afternoon sun spilled through the window, bathing the room in a golden light.

Maggie gazed at her, Alice's bleak expression tugging at her heartstrings. She fought to keep her concern from showing as the teenager looked up.

Maggie smiled. "Hi."

"Hi." Alice took off the headphones. "She's gone."

"Yes. Can I come in?" Alice nodded and Maggie stepped into the room, closing the door behind her.

"You look happy."

"I am. She's not going to try to take Manda away. It's going to be all right."

"I'm glad for you." Alice plucked at the pillowcase. "She's a neat little girl."

"I've got more good news."

Alice searched her expression, her own expression cautious. "You have?"

"Mmm, hmm." Maggie crossed the room and sank onto the edge of the bed. The anxiety in Alice's eyes and the memory of their argument on Christmas Eve made her choose her words carefully. "But I want you to be okay about this. I want us to talk about it."

"You and Mr. Royce are getting back together, aren't you?"

Maggie smiled and shook her head. "You're always a step ahead of me, Alice. Yes, we're getting back together. And this time we're going to make it."

"You're sure?"

"Positive."

"Oh." Alice lowered her head, toying with the pillowcase again. "Great."

"Alice?" The teenager wouldn't look at her, and Maggie bit back a sigh. "I meant what I said. What you think is important to me."

"I told you," she whispered. "It's great."

"You don't look like you think it's great. You don't sound that way, either." Maggie reached out and with her fingertips tilted Alice's face up to hers. "Why don't you tell me what's wrong. What happened today?"

"Mr. Royce didn't tell you?"

Alice's eyes glistened with unshed tears, and Maggie shook her head. "No. But maybe you should."

For a moment Maggie thought Alice would refuse, then she let out a shuddering breath and began. She told Maggie about getting caught shoplifting and about Royce coming to get her. She told her what she'd taken and assured her, as she had Royce, that she wouldn't do it again.

"Is that all you have to tell me?" Maggie asked quietly when Alice finished.

Alice peeked up at her, then averted her gaze again. "No," she whispered, twisting the edge of the floral pillowcase between her fingers.

"What else, Alice? Talk to me."

A moment of silence stretched between them, then Alice looked up, her eyes brimming with tears. "I wished Amanda would go away," she whispered. "I wished she'd just disappear. And then . . . when it looked like . . ."

Alice drew in a deep, shuddering breath and lifted her gaze pleadingly to Maggie's. "I didn't mean it. I swear I didn't. I never wanted you to be unhappy, Maggie. When it looked like my wish was coming true, I prayed you wouldn't lose her. I prayed so hard. Please forgive me."

Alice clasped her hands together. "If you let me stay I promise I won't think anything like that again. Please don't send me away."

She burst into tears and Maggie eased her into her arms. Softly stroking her hair, she murmured, "You can't wish things to happen, Alice. And you didn't think anything every other sister or brother hasn't thought before." She laughed lightly. "In fact, many a time I wished one of my brothers or sisters would disappear. And usually it was Louise."

"Louise?" she repeated incredulously.

"Mmm, hmm. Sharing can be a real pain sometimes." Alice rested her head against her shoulder. Maggie stroked her hair. "What does concern me, Alice, is why you think I would send you away."

She sniffled. "Well, you and Mr. Royce are getting back together. And you have Amanda now."

So why would you want me?

Alice's words, the question, hung unspoken in the air between them, and Maggie tightened her arms around the teenager. "It's I who should ask forgiveness, Alice. I shut you out. I shut Royce out. I let myself be consumed by fear. Because of my past I was certain Manda was going to be taken away. And oddly I felt I deserved that pain. So I closed myself off from the people who cared about me, the people who could have helped me."

She tilted Alice's face up to hers. "Do you understand?"

The teenager searched her expression, then nodded solemnly. "I do. I feel that way a lot."

"And it's wrong, Alice. We deserve as much happiness as anybody else. The people who mistreated us did so not because they couldn't love us but because they couldn't love themselves."

She brushed at the tears on Alice's cheeks with her thumbs. "You mean an awful lot to me, Alice. You're part of my family. Part of my life." She smiled softly. "If I promise never to be so selfish and insensitive and silly again, will you stay?"

Alice threw her arms around her. "I love you so much, Maggie. When I thought you didn't need me around anymore, I wanted to die I hurt so bad."

Maggie clung to her, moved not only by Alice's words, but by the fact that she had revealed herself. For one who had been rejected so often and so painfully, opening up, chancing rejection again, took boundless courage. And a loving heart.

"I love you, too," Maggie whispered back. She pulled away in order to look into Alice's eyes. "If you ever get to feeling unimportant again, come talk to me. I want us to always be able to talk. Okay?"

Alice wiped her eyes and hiccuped. "Okay."

Maggie touched Alice's hair, now grown into a short, smooth bob. "Could you watch Manda for a while? Royce and I have some talking to do ourselves."

"Everything's okay? I mean, he is going to stay?"

"Yes." Maggie smiled at the glimmer of eagerness in the girl's eyes. "You're okay about that?"

"Yeah." Alice shrugged in attempted indifference. "He's pretty cool."

"Can I quote you on that?"

Color crept up her cheeks. "I think I'll tell him myself."

They both stood. Laughing, Maggie linked her arm through Alice's and they headed downstairs.

Royce and Amanda were having a high time playing airplane in the parlor, but he gladly turned her over
to Alice anyway. The teenager asked if she could bundle the infant up and stroll over to the coffeehouse to
see Aunt Louise, and Maggie agreed. At that moment there was nothing she wanted more than to have
the house to herself and Royce.

After Alice left, Maggie grasped Royce's hand and
led him to their bedroom. She shut the door behind
them, then turned back to him, breathless with wanting. "There's so much I want to say to you," she
murmured, loosening his tie. "But I don't want to talk
now."

"No?"

"No," she repeated and tossed the tie aside. She
started to work on his shirt buttons then, easing one
after another through the buttonholes. "The three
days I've been without you seemed a lifetime."

"How did we go nine months before?"

"Pure idiocy." She yanked the tails of his shirt from
the waistband of his trousers. "Which we can discuss—"

"Later," he murmured for her, pushing her cardigan from her shoulders and going to work on the buttons of her silk blouse.

"Mmm, hmm." She pressed her mouth to his chest
and nipped, then soothed the spot with her tongue.
"You taste delicious."

Royce laughed softly. "I thought you didn't want to
talk." He slipped the last button through its hole; her
blouse slithered to the floor.

"I forgot..." He mimicked her, kissing, nipping, soothing. "I mean—" she curled her fingers around his shoulders and arched her back "—I don't..."

So they didn't. Instead, they undressed one another. Slowly, carefully. Reverently. Each touch, each murmured sigh, an expression of their newfound—and rediscovered—love for one another.

Royce carried her to the bed; they fell onto it. Holding, caressing, whispering one another's names, Royce sank into her. Their lovemaking was slow and sweet; together they achieved new heights of tenderness.

As they reached the brink and tumbled over it, Maggie knew she would never be wanting again. The tiny void inside her, the one that neither Amanda nor Royce had been able to fill, now brimmed over. She'd always loved others, but now she loved herself as well.

Once and for all, she'd put her past behind her. Smiling, she pressed her mouth to Royce's damp shoulder. Now, this moment, she started anew.

Maggie threaded her fingers through his hair. But first, before she could completely shut the door to the past, she wanted, needed, to share everything she'd realized with her husband.

"Royce?"

Still holding her, Royce rolled onto his side so they faced one another. "Hmm?"

"I want to apologize to you." She took a deep breath. "I want you to understand why I behaved as I did these past few days—and over a year ago. I want you to understand why I pushed you away. I only realized myself today."

"You don't have to," he murmured, trailing a hand over the curve of her hip. "I don't need to hear the words."

"But I need to say them." She sat up and pulled the sheet around her. "I was always terrified of losing you. From the moment we married—before that, even. Because I loved you so much, because as a child I'd . . . always lost what I loved."

She plucked at the coverlet. "And then my fears started to become reality. Our marriage began to disintegrate. Even so, I couldn't let go of my obsessive need for a baby." She met his eyes. "It was wrong, what I did. In a marriage decisions have to be shared. One party can't bulldoze the other. But I was too wrapped up in my own emotions to see that then."

He laced her fingers with his. "I became the bad guy."

She held tightly on to his hand. "Not completely. I told myself you were. I told myself I was better off without a man who didn't have love enough for a child. But I still loved you."

Maggie brought their joined hands to her mouth. "I was trying to atone for something I had no part in. It was as if, by becoming a mother and being a wonderful one, I could somehow undo the events and the pain of my own childhood." She shook her head, smiling softly. "A seventeen-year-old girl helped me see that before I even had an inkling."

"Alice."

Maggie nodded. "The threat of losing Manda helped me see, too. When I finally snapped out of my grief." She kissed his hand once more, then brought it back to her lap. "When it all started falling apart, back then and three days ago, it was my mother leaving me all over again. I felt rejected and unloved and unworthy. And both times I completed the cycle by forcing you out of my life. Back then with the ultimatum about Alice, and recently by shutting you out."

She looked back up at him, tears welling in her eyes. "I didn't mean those hateful things I said, Royce. I know you love Amanda, I knew it before you told Sarah today."

Royce pulled her back down to him. "You could never force me out of your life, Maggie. Even the nine months we were separated, I wasn't out of your life. I thought of you every day, every minute."

"And I you."

Royce cupped her cheek in his hand. "You don't have the corner on explanations, you know. It took both of us to make our marriage and both of us to tear it down. All my life I felt like I was on the outside looking in. Wanting affection, wanting that elusive, unattainable something called love. Then I found you and suddenly I had 'it.'"

He smiled and trailed his thumb ever so gently across her cheekbone. "But your need for a family— your family itself—made me feel on the outside again. I felt alienated. And afraid. Of losing you, of losing 'it.' Those feelings helped drive us apart."

"I didn't know, Royce. I—"

"How could you? I didn't know myself." He tangled his fingers in her hair, rubbing the velvety black strands between his fingers. "It's ironic that when I came back, what had driven us apart pulled me back in. I was drawn to your magic circle. Alice and Amanda. And you. I wanted my family. I realized suddenly what it was to have one. Really have one.

"You tried to recreate your past, and so did I." He laughed lightly. "Maybe, to a certain extent, everyone does. Until someone or something comes along and forces a change. I thank God for you and Amanda and Alice. And Sarah."

Royce tightened his fingers in Maggie's hair and gazed deeply into her eyes. "You all forced me to change. To realize I wasn't my parents. To realize not only that I was loved, without strings, but that I was capable of giving love. To you. To a child. You asked me once why I let you bulldoze about children. It was because I felt so damn guilty. I felt like a sponge who sucked up your love and gave nothing in return."

"Oh, Royce, that's just not true—"

He laid his fingers gently over her lips. "I know that now. And I also know that all along I loved you desperately. As you said to Sarah today, to love so much, so completely is a terrifying thing. But to feel nothing is more terrifying still."

He brushed his lips lightly across hers. "I love you." He caught her lips again, this time with more heat. "I love Amanda."

He found her mouth again, deeply. When he pulled away, she was breathless. "I want us to be a family. I want Alice to be with us, too. She's an incredible person. She has so much love to give . . . and such a need to give it."

He laughed and shook his head. "I thought I'd been a fool to believe in you...to believe in love, but I see now, I'd been a fool not to. Never again, my love. Never again."

Maggie smiled up at him. "I love you, Royce Adler."

"I love you, Maggie Ryan Adler." His mouth covered hers again.

From below, they heard a slam, excited squeals and laughter.

Maggie lifted her head. "Tell me that's not what I think it is."

Royce groaned and flopped back against the pillow. "If I do, will you believe me?"

"Not a chance." She propped herself on an elbow and grinned down at him. "What do you say? Ready to go downstairs and be a family...Daddy?"

Royce paused a moment, then returned her grin. "Call me that again."

"Daddy?"

"Yeah." His grin became a full-fledged smile. "Not that long ago I wondered how it would feel to be called that."

"And?" Maggie asked, although she already knew.

"It feels good. Great, in fact." He dipped his head and caught her mouth in a brief but smoldering kiss. When he pulled away, his eyes danced with wicked amusement. "Come on, Mommy. Our family awaits."

* * * * *

NORA ROBERTS

Love has a language all its own, and for centuries, flowers have symbolized love's finest expression. Discover the language of flowers—and love—in this romantic collection of 48 favorite books by bestselling author Nora Roberts.

Starting in February, two titles will be available each month at your favorite retail outlet.

In March, look for:

Irish Rose, Volume #3
Storm Warning, Volume #4

In April, look for:

First Impressions, Volume #5
Reflections, Volume #6

Collect all 48 titles and become fluent in

THE LANGUAGE of LOVE

LOL392

Silhouette Special Edition

salutes

MOMENTS OF GLORY

from Lindsay McKenna

In a country torn with conflict, in a time of bitter passions, these brave men and women wage a war against all odds... and a timeless battle for honor, for fleeting moments of glory, for the promise of enduring love.

February: RIDE THE TIGER (#721) Survivor Dany Villard is wise to the love-'em-and-leave-'em ways of war, but wounded hero Gib Ramsey swears she's captured his heart... forever.

March: ONE MAN'S WAR (#727) The war raging inside brash and bold Captain Pete Mallory threatens to destroy him, until Tess Ramsey's tender love guides him toward peace.

April: OFF LIMITS (#733) Soft-spoken Marine Jim McKenzie saved Alexandra Vance's life in Vietnam; now he needs her love to save his honor....